The Final
of
Abbot Montrose

Sven Elvestad

Originally Published as *Montrose* in 1917

Kazabo Publishing

Translation and Foreword © 2018 Kazabo Publishing

Garamond 22/16/12

ISBN: 978-1-948104-15-9

All rights reserved.

Kazabo Publishing

Kazabo.com

Kazabo books are available at special discounts when purchased in bulk or by book clubs. Special editions of many of our books can also be created for promotional and educational use. Please visit us at kazabo.com for more information.

Table of Contents

Foreword

Sven Elvestad – who also wrote as Stein Riverton – is a pivotal figure in European detective fiction. Born in Norway in 1884, he wrote – and published – his first detective story at seventeen. In addition to being an author, he was also an active journalist well known for his exploits: He once spent an entire day in a lion's cage and he was probably the first foreign reporter to interview Adolf Hitler. All in all, he wrote over 90 books as well as countless articles, essays and short stories.

Elvestad himself was a complicated character and almost everything the caricature of the moderate, sober Scandinavian is not. He was larger-than-life, both in stature (and girth) as well as in his habits, and a widely traveled bon-vivant who thoroughly enjoyed the pleasure of food, drink and tobacco.

Though Elvestad died in 1934, some of his literary creations have long outlived him. Much like Sherlock Holmes, one of his characters, Detective Knut Gribb, is still featured in new stories and films today even though Elvestad created him over 100 years ago.

Which brings us to Asbjørn Krag, the hero of *The Final Days of Abbot Montrose*. Asbjørn Krag was probably Elvestad's favorite protagonist. While Elvestad wrote about other characters as well, Krag features in a plurality of his novels. Elvestad is widely credited as the inventor of the Norwegian police procedural and Krag usually appears with a partner. But while his partner is a thoroughly respectable police detective, methodical and diligent, Krag is an artist, capable of both brilliant reasoning and flashes of insight. While Krag himself is given to neither boasting nor display, he is portrayed as being "world famous" and is often mentioned in the newspapers to the annoyance of his colleague.

Asbjørn Krag also features in *Jernvognen* (published in English as *The Iron Chariot*) which is one of Elvestad's most famous works in part because *Jernvognen* anticipates a literary device that Agatha Christie would later use in *The Murder of Roger Ackroyd*.

It is no surprise, given his immense and varied literary output, that Elvestad's work could be uneven. But in Scandinavia and Germany, his best novels are considered to be some of the best detective fiction ever written. In Norway, Elvestad wrote much of his crime fiction under the name "Stein Riverton" and, even today, The Riverton prize is awarded annually to the best Norwegian crime story.

Apart from being known for his clever and intricate plots, Elvestad had a capacity for observation and description which is quite remarkable. Consider his description of a crowd that gathers at the scene of a murder.

> There were people of all ages, the sort of crowd that always gathers when something serious has happened— a conflagration, a crime, or an accident of some sort. There stood the barefoot urchin with his spin top, serious, and yet vacant, with his mouth hanging open, surrounded by little children who barely dared to whisper to each other; red-cheeked women, their fat, bare arms folded across their chests; workers from the new building nearby, some with their tools in hand, others without hats, proof of the haste with which they had left their work. One saw the types of passersby, as one usually encounters in crowds on the street: the fine gray-bearded gentleman with the top hat, who had been out for a walk; the telegraph messenger, who has gotten off his bike; the distraught old lady, who has already taken out her handkerchief; the man in the wheelchair relentlessly left to his fate—all mingling without distinction into a whispering, frightened, questioning crowd.

Elvestad enjoyed writing enormously and it shows. When he lets himself off the leash, buckle your seatbelt and hold on because you are going for a wild ride. In this novel, there is one section in particular, in which Elvestad describes the thoughts and impressions of a murderer approaching a house, that qualifies as the literary equivalent of a roller coaster. This passage, which is too lengthy to quote here, may not be to everyone's taste but it is something that could easily have been written by Edgar Allan Poe.

While some might challenge Elvestad's gift for description as "purple prose," I disagree. These passages are written with a purpose and it strikes me that they achieve that purpose admirably. In particular, the passage describing a murder's thoughts and impressions is written as it is to create a very specific effect, both within the story and within one of the characters.

Many of Elvestad's books also incorporate a surprising amount of commentary and symbolism without ever distracting from the story itself. *The Final Days of Abbot Montrose* is no exception.

In 1933, Aksel Sandemose, then living in Norway, wrote a book entitled, *A Fugitive Crosses His Tracks* in which he defined what came to be known as "The Law of Jante." "Jante Law" described a set of social attitudes built around the idea that "You are not to think you are anything special." These rules are certainly "repressive" in that they sacrifice individuality in pursuit of the greater good but they are generally accepted even today as one of the cornerstones of Scandinavian society.

Sandemose did not invent these laws in 1933. Rather, he merely put a name to attitudes and trends that had been dominant in Scandinavia for many years. Elvestad wrote *The Final Days of Abbot Montrose* in 1917, 16 years earlier, and it seems clear he was aware of – and struggled with – the same issues. Elvestad was something of a character as well as one of the most famous writers in Scandinavia. He was, therefore, a very tall nail who resolutely refused to be hammered down and this book reflects that. While on one level it's an excellent story, on another level, Elvestad is offering a commentary on the society in which he lived. The Abbey is perfectly respectable and composed, a highly-admired vision of tranquility and harmony. But just next door to the Abbey is the Krydder district, the home of misfits, characters and criminals. In particular, it is home to The Gilded Peacock, an extraordinary, thoroughly "disreputable" hotel where anything can, and does, happen.

Apparently, the hotel had grown several times. The floors were stacked, like boxes messily glued together. The various builders, who at different times had enlarged this building, had taken no account of form or proportion; where they found space, they built a quadrangle and connected it to the old building with cleverly laid-out staircases and angular corridors. Corridors and stairs ran like mole's paths across the whole building. Down three flights of stairs and then down a section of corridor, up four flights of stairs, a narrow corridor with a sharp bend, then three staircases, and again a corridor dividing into several corridors, and again narrow corridors and new stairs.

From time to time the footsteps of the three men called forth a faint, metallic ringing sound that betrayed that the corridor was over a passageway below. The corridors, however, were covered with rugs that muffled their steps. On the wall panels between the doors, all in a red hue reminiscent of old blood, were painted fantastic animals, many of which belonged to some unreal world. A basilisk showed its terrifying eyes, a sea serpent snaked dangerously around the door jambs, and huge fairytale birds spread their wings far above the ceiling. Two kinds of animals, however, kept returning: a peacock, with its graceful splendor expressing indescribable well-being, and a monkey dangling from its tail, showing a grim but human face.

To make the confusion even greater, the doors had no sequential numbers, but the numbers were arranged according to a particular, and yet incomprehensible, system.

As the story develops – which I will not give away here! – it is hard not to view this as a commentary on Norwegian society. The Abbey is the respectable face which everyone must show their neighbors while The Gilded Peacock is a person's secret, inner life. What happens in The Gilded Peacock stays in The Gilded Peacock . . . until it doesn't. And when it doesn't, there must be a reckoning.

Almost ninety years ago, Elvestad's immense success in Scandinavia and Germany earned the attention of no less than Dashiell Hammett, who said of Elvestad, "Here is work for translators." Despite that endorsement, very little of his work has been translated into English. After reading *The Final Days of Abbot Montrose*, we hope you will agree that this is an error that deserves correction.

Chiara Giacobbe

I. A Spring Night

Policeman Number 314 put his police whistle in his pocket, stood motionless, and peered down the street. It was about three o'clock in the morning, a very quiet spring night and quite dark. The sky was covered with black clouds. It had rained recently, and the air was saturated with a stunning floral scent from the gardens. Neither the sounds of carts rolling nor footsteps could be heard. The paved road rose gently and disappeared on the horizon. On both sides of the street stood villas, half buried under the fragrant blossoms of the fruit trees. No light shone in the windows. The policeman was still listening as he watched a certain part of the road, which was bordered by a tall and elegant wrought-iron fence. Beyond it, the silhouette of a slender church tower stood out among the darkened crowns of the trees. Other parts of a building were also visible between the trees, the glimmer of a beautiful façade, fragments of cornices and a piece of a wall. From out here it looked as if a great mansion or an old castle was dreaming in the silence of the garden behind the dense iron bars of the fence.

At last footsteps sounded further down the street, hasty footsteps approaching, and the listening policeman nodded with satisfaction. A man came running. Shortly after, he appeared out of the shadows of the trees. It was a second policeman.

"Hurry up," cried Number 314. "Something's happened."

"I heard your signal," answered the other breathlessly. "So, what's going on?"

This policeman had "12" in shiny brass numbers on his uniform cap.

Number 314 pointed to the fence.

"In there," he replied as he pulled the other man with him, "shouting, noise, and shattering glass."

"My goodness!" gasped Number 12 in astonishment. "In there?"

The two policemen stopped in front of the great gate of artfully forged iron between massive granite pedestals, which formed the entrance to the property. Of course, the gate was locked.

Number 314 thought for a few seconds, and to avoid wasting time with unnecessary explanations he said aloud, "It is better," he said, "to climb over the railing than to walk around the house to the other street." (The large property spread between two streets like a park.)

Number 12 was of the same opinion, and like skilled gymnasts they quickly climbed over the bars. They made as little noise as possible, yet they could not prevent a loud crackling as they jumped down from the fence into the dense bushes. Without thinking, they continued toward the building, now more clearly visible in the back of the garden.

"Quick, quick!" cried Number 314 as he raced on. As they ran they heard a new noise of voices and broken windows.

"Do you hear that?" called Number 12.

"Yes," said the other.

"They're cursing. In such a place, huh! Now they've run away." Rattling and the sound of hurried footsteps running in the opposite direction, the cracking of branches and twigs could be heard in the distance. Number 314 put the police whistle to his mouth and signaled desultorily. Then everything became quiet. The policemen knew that the other road was unpaved. You could walk there silently on the soft ground. The perpetrators, whoever they were, had probably already moved to safety in the neighborhood's many alleys.

The policemen had now reached the main door. Again Number 314 thought out loud. It was clear to him that a burglary had taken place. A broken window with broken glass hung loosely on its hinges and creaked miserably. Inside, a restless but weak fire flickered. The fire decided him.

"Climb through the window and see what's going on inside," he said to Number 12. "I'll check outside in the meantime."

As the other policeman climbed in through the open window, Number 314 ran through the garden to catch, if possible, another glimpse of the criminals. But everything was completely quiet again. He could clearly follow their path over the crushed flower beds and past the broken branches. When he came to the bars of the fence, he saw a dark piece of cloth fluttering from an iron bar. He climbed up and took it. It was a tattered piece of a vestment, the type the Catholic priests wore.

Number 314 sat atop the fence and peered around. But there was not a living being anywhere to be seen. The road was empty and silent. The dawning spring morning threw a faint glow into the little street and flashed on windows and shop signs.

"There in the tangle of streets," thought Number 314, "they are hiding." And he sighed, knowing that for the time being it would be hopeless to seek out the criminals in the chaos of the big city, where the roads crossed like cracks in old mud.

After vainly examining the garden along the fence and finding no more evidence he returned to his colleague with the piece of cloth in his hand. If Number 314 had had the slightest sense of natural beauty, the wonderful calm and the spring-like silence that reigned over the noise in the garden would have touched his heart. The trees leaned tall and immobile over the white garden paths; the flower beds, which were still damp after the evening rain, wafted soft fragrances. Lounge chairs made of light wickerwork stood in a gazebo of dense wild grapevines, a blanket hung carelessly over the back of a chair. Deeper in the garden, above the trees, stood the tower of a small red brick church—and just in front of Number 314 was the main house where the break-in had taken place. It was a delightful little half-timbered building surrounded by flower beds of white and blue spring flowers, the walls were covered by the thick green of the climbing plants and above the roof hovered cherry tree crowns like fragrant clouds. The whole area, from the church spire to the fence bars, seemed to express nothing but a strange, gentle calm, into which the memory of the screaming and the noise of the splintered windowpanes sounded senselessly inappropriate. None of this, however, touched Number 314 as he strode toward the low, half-timbered building. His mind contained only the driest of calculations, "Burglary ten minutes to three o'clock," he was already thinking of the report. And intelligent as he was, he was thinking at the same time of the objections that would be made, "Why," he would probably be asked at the police department, "Why didn't one of them go to the other side of the house?" "That's why," he wanted to answer, because even at the quickest pace, it would have taken no less than five minutes to get around the house. And from the moment the policemen reached the fence until the thieves disappeared, barely two minutes had passed. That's what Number 314 thought.

When he came near the house, the wide door was torn open and, in the doorway, stood Number 12.

"No one's here," said Number 12, "not a living soul."

Something strange in his voice, however, awoke Number 314's attention and he stopped on the garden path. The morning grew brighter and brighter. The blue police uniforms were in sharp contrast to the yellow earth. The voices of the police officers sounded almost sharply metallic.

"Did you see anything?" asked Number 314.

"It looks terrible inside," replied Number 12. "Everything has been thrown upside-down. And there is blood everywhere."

"But the fire?"

"The fire is extinguished."

Number 314 went on. The soil crunched under his heavy boots.

This took place on 2nd of May in the garden of the Catholic abbey. The church, whose tower and roof were visible among the trees, was a small Catholic church within a great Protestant city.

And the house in the garden belonged to the scholar, Abbot Montrose.

II. While Keller Dictates

An hour later—as life in the city began to awaken with the day's first eager footsteps on the pavement, the lively whinnying of horses, and rolling wagons—there was a tumult in Abbot Montrose's study.

There were several people at the scene.

In addition to our old friends, Numbers 12 and 314, there was a middle-aged gentleman in a light spring coat with his collar turned up, as if he was cold on that glorious spring morning. This gentleman yawned several times, and perhaps he really was cold, for fatigue, as we know, lowers the body temperature. He expressed his impatience by staying near the door. He looked as if he was thinking, "Why on earth am I here? I belong in my bed." This man was the medical examiner.

Next to Abbot Montrose's large desk stood an indescribable person. That is, he was indescribable in that he didn't have any special characteristics about him. He was a man like Gogol's heroes in *Dead Souls*, neither bright nor dark, neither fat nor thin, a very ordinary person—someone you think you've seen before, even when meeting him only for the first time. He could be a merchant or a civil servant, but he is a detective employed by the police department. He has the perfect appearance for a detective in that he never, and nowhere, stands out from his surroundings; he is a person who disappears into the crowd, loses himself in the colorless mass. His name is Keller.

Next to him in front of the desk, pen in hand, policeman Number 12 sits and writes slowly and carefully, following Keller's dictation. Keller occasionally looks around at various items in the room, as if he is about to make an inventory. Once he turns to the medical examiner with the following question, "Are you sure, doctor, that these red spots are blood?"

"Yes," says the medical examiner, "there is no doubt about that."

"So," Keller continues in his dictation, "a blanket stained with blood, a red and yellow scarf, also stained with blood . . ."

"Also . . . stained . . . wi . . . th . . . bl . . . ood," murmurs Number 12 as he writes.

In a deep and comfortable armchair sits a silent gentleman who seems to be interested only in the tips of his boots. He looks down at them continuously, so that his bald head stands out brightly from the dark leather of the chair. His face is thin and pale, but with strong features and a slightly graying, short-cropped mustache. His chin, which now rests on his black tie, is unusually wide and strong.

Number 314 is standing next to the desk and eating his buttered bread with slow deliberation. Nothing prevents a policeman from eating his sandwich in the evening. Often lonesome souls walking at night can hear paper rustling from a darkened gateway, that's the policeman eating his sandwich. In many quiet cities nothing happens over the long nights at all except that the policeman eats his sandwich. For the moment, Number 314 had nothing special to do, so he'd pulled out his sandwich. As uncomplicated natures are, it never occurred to Number 314 that it was odd how he stood and chewed here on the scene of a bloody drama.

Because the large room bore the unmistakable signs of terrible violence.

They were in the Abbot's library and study, decorated in a stylish, cultivated manner that showed both culture and wealth. The many books that almost completely covered the one long wall were all expensively bound. There were pieces of antique furniture and old pictures and on the carpet lay the sad remains of a fine porcelain vase. The intruders had dealt badly with this beautiful room. Furniture had been overturned, books ripped from their covers, paper strewn everywhere, and the large desk was stained with ink and blood. A mahogany cabinet had been broken completely, and the drawers were on the floor. The shattered window hung loosely on its hinges and rattled in the morning breeze.

We have met Number 314 and Number 12 so far, as well as the medical examiner and Detective Keller. But who was the gentleman gazing at the tips of his boots, the silent gentleman who looked as if he was between scenes and waiting for his cue in a play?

We will find out immediately, because it turns out that the man with the fascinating boot tips is not an uninterested observer at all, but that on the contrary he has been following Keller's dictation with the utmost attention. When Keller reaches the following in his inventory, "The photograph of a young lady—"

—The gentleman lifts his gaze from his boots and says, "From?"

"From?" Keller asks in astonishment. "What do you mean, Mr. Krag?"

"From Arendorff's studio," the other man continues and gets up. "If the list is to be accurate, you must not forget the smallest details."

Asbjörn Krag, the famous detective, went into the garden and the medical examiner followed him while the other policemen continued their work. Krag could still be considered a young man with his lithe figure. But his peculiar face with the deep lines around his mouth, the very fine lines on his eyes behind his pince-nez, and the bald white forehead, seemed to indicate that he was already past middle age.

Nevertheless, Krag was only forty years old.

"What do you think?" The medical examiner asked, yawning. Crime scenes were old and familiar to him.

"I think it's a lovely morning," replied the detective, crossing his arms taking a deep breath of the fragrant air.

"No, I mean about the events in there," said the doctor.

8

"You can see that for yourself," answered Krag, "burglary, plunder, robbery, whatever you want to call it. I suppose Abbot Montrose had many valuables in the broken mahogany cabinet."

"There have been several criminals here."

"Without a doubt. One of them was most likely a sailor. "

"My goodness, how do you know that?"

Krag turned to the doctor and showed his strong teeth in a good-natured smile.

"I remembered a verse from a shanty," replied the detective, "which begins:

> In bright Spanish colors,

> In colors of red and yellow—

I have been thinking about this verse constantly for the last half hour."

"I don't understand you," said the doctor in a low voice. "Do you think a murder has been committed? All the blood—"

"Yes, blood is everywhere," replied the detective evasively.

"Anyway, a life-and-death struggle has taken place."

"Without doubt."

"But where is Abbot Montrose?"

"Disappeared," said Krag, "but he was present."

"Tonight, during the fight?"

"Certainly."

The doctor shivered as if he felt an icy breeze.

"It would be sad," he said, "if a misfortune has befallen him, such a noble personality, such a truly outstanding scholar . . . Do you think he was killed?"

"It's not impossible," said the detective.

"And his body taken?"

"That would be a curious idea," Krag muttered.

"One of the policemen found a scrap of the Abbot's vestments on the fence, on the path the criminals have taken in their flight—"

"Quite right," said Krag, "and the Abbot is nowhere to be found. The whole thing is strange."

"And frightening?" the doctor asked uncertainly.

Krag nodded.

"And frightening," he confirmed.

A gentle wind moved the trees of the garden, the foliage rustled, it sounded like a distant surf. Krag stopped, stared broodingly, and the medical examiner heard him mumble, "He will not come back . . . maybe he will not come back—"

The detective stared thoughtfully into the distance, as if expecting someone or something, a person, or a landmark to appear among the mighty, rolling crowns of the trees and come to him through the foliage with the morning light.

The big city awoke more and more. The noise of the day had replaced the night's silence.

III. The Photograph

The Daily Newspaper, which came out earliest on Saturday, was the first newspaper to give a detailed account of the strange events. The newspaper covered the incident quite extensively, and there was no doubt in the opinion of the editors that a strange and ugly crime had been committed. The newspaper emphasized the mysterious disappearance of Abbot Montrose.

Here are some excerpts from the manuscript of the report:

The crime was committed between two and three o'clock last night. Judging by the footprints in the garden, at least three, but probably more people, have been involved in the crime. They apparently intended to plunder Abbot Montrose's apartment, where they expected to find expensive valuables. The wrongdoers were not mistaken. Abbot Montrose is widely known as a very wealthy man who had an aesthetic predilection for old jewelry and probably had a large collection. He kept some of it in his library in a four-hundred-year-old Venetian cabinet. This cabinet was broken and its contents have disappeared. It has also been established that the day before the crime the Abbot had withdrawn the sum of ten thousand kroner from the bank, with which he intended to pay the Catholic Hospital's weekly bills. Abbot Montrose was the treasurer of the hospital. The payments normally took place on Saturday. The fact that the crime was committed on Friday night may be a sign to the police that the criminals must be sought among those who were familiar with the Abbot's habits. The money is also missing.

"Abbot Montrose," the newspaper went on:

. . . had his bedroom next to the library. He was probably awakened by the noise the criminals made while breaking open the antique Venetian cabinet. And here, the first mysterious circumstance appears. Instead of rushing straight into the next room and chasing away the thieves, Abbot Montrose took some time to get dressed and didn't enter the library until he had thrown his priest's cassock over his clothing. Perhaps it was the Abbot's intention to impress the criminals with his religious authority. What happened next is unclear. It appears that one of the criminals may have been smoking a pipe and may have thrown it down in shock at the appearance of the Abbot in his vestments. The burning pipe set fire to the carpet, which was eventually extinguished by the police. The traces of blood and the condition of the room prove that a terrible fight has taken place. While he was a very reserved man, Abbot Montrose managed, in the short time he was the head of the Catholic abbey, to earn the highest reputation for his charity and for his great scientific scholarship. We regret that it appears that this highly esteemed man has probably been the victim of a violent crime. At the same time, however, we must point out the mystery surrounding this bizarre crime. The strangest thing is the fact that the criminals had the time to abduct the Abbot— dead or alive. The purpose of this abduction remains an unanswered question for the police who are actively investigating this strange matter.

"As of the print deadline"—this is how the presentation ends—"we don't yet know anything about the Abbot. The last vestige of the missing priest is a scrap of his robes, which the police found on the iron bars of the garden fence."

This article was read by Asbjörn Krag as he sat on the windowsill in Detective Keller's office. After reading it, he put the newspaper aside and turned to the window. The offices of the police department opened onto a large square where several streets met and where the city traffic was noisy. Krag was alone in the room, but he seemed to be waiting for someone because he looked impatiently at his watch several times. Finally, the door opened, and Keller came in.

Keller handed Krag a piece of paper, "For some reason, Abbot Montrose made his notes on tiny scraps of paper. I found several."

While Krag read the note, Keller immersed himself in the newspaper Krag had put aside.

The piece of paper Keller had given Krag was torn from a small writing pad, and read, "Have paid gardener S. thirty kroner for six working days." Then came the date: May 1st.

"That exonerates the gardener," said Krag, "but we should still keep him in custody."

"Of course," replied Keller, looking up from the newspaper. "It seems the newspaper doesn't yet know about the arrest and that's good. These damn talkative reporters always spoil the game for us. But the Abbot is still gone and the fear in the community is great. Mary, his old housekeeper, cried all morning. I've just gotten a report from the search party. There are no traces; the whole Krydder District has been searched." The Krydder District was the name for a troubled and chaotic neighborhood where a hundred thousand more or less dubious individuals lived and which was adjacent to the wealthy district where the Catholic abbey had its church, hospital, and large garden.

Keller hit his knee with the folded newspaper.

"If only I could understand," he said, "what is the purpose of the abduction of the priest. Dead or alive, they dragged him along. What on earth do the criminals want to achieve? Is it blackmail? Kidnapping?"

"Why abduct Abbot Montrose, who has neither family nor friends?" Krag said. "And if the criminals killed him, you cannot make money out of a dead man."

"No, exactly. But then why all these circumstances? Remember, the criminals dragged him over the garden fence and into the Krydder District. Isn't it strange that no one witnessed this unusual spectacle? What do you want to do now? Continue to deal with the detainee?"

"No," said Krag, "I'll leave him alone for now. I expect a message from the port. I can't get the old shanty about the bright Spanish colors out of my head."

13

This conversation between the two detectives took place at about one o'clock in the afternoon. The conversation revealed that something important had happened: an arrest had been made. This arrest was still a secret to the public.

And what had happened?

Just this: Asbjörn Krag and Keller had sent everyone away after the crime scene report had been completed. Then the two detectives had tried to understand between them what, exactly, among the pile of evidence might be significant. More than enough clues had been left.

Krag had said, "One thing is certain: the criminals have been surprised. A fierce fight has taken place, most likely between them and the Abbot. He defended himself well. This is indicated by the appearance of the room and the things that the criminals lost in the heat of the battle. These items, the scarf, the photograph, the tobacco pouch, etc., also reveal that the criminals were likely to be among the vermin hiding in the Krydder District. Several of these things were clear leads, especially the photograph."

"It's the photograph of a young lady," continued Krag, "one of those pretty, sympathetic, young girls you find by the thousands in the city's cigar or fashionable clothing stores. She's probably the wife or girlfriend of one of the criminals and is called something like Annie, or Dolly, or Polly. The photograph is, at the moment, the best signpost we have pointing to the perpetrators. So, let us follow the signpost.

"On the back of the photograph is the name and address of the studio, apart from the number 2007 and the typical photographer's notice, 'The photographic plate is kept for re-orders.' Furthermore, the photograph is rather dirty and seems to have been carried by the owner in his pocket for a long time. A close examination will likely reveal fingerprints and other features."

All this was the reason why the photographer, Arendorff, had been summoned out of bed at six o'clock in the morning and asked to accompany the two gentlemen to his studio. A minute later it became

14

clear that the photograph portrayed the wife of Arnold Singer, 28 Hussars Way.

At seven o'clock, Krag and Keller were in front of 28 Hussars Way. Here they came across a man to whom they showed the photograph, and who said, "This is my wife's picture and the photograph is mine."

The details of the encounter between the detectives and this man were such that they would have the greatest importance for the development of this strange case.

That is why it is necessary to go into more detail about what happened, from the moment the detectives left the drowsy photographer's studio to the meeting with the man on Hussars Way.

IV. Murder

Here, it must be said that Hussars Way wasn't part of the Krydder District, on the contrary, Hussars Way was part of a large, new quarter that formed the link between city and the countryside to the east. There, a caring city government had provided one of the large community meadows for development—following the most modern principles— to house the lower middle class. In a short time, a lovely garden district had sprung up in the large area—street after street of small homes, surrounded by well-tended gardens. The streets were given military names to honor the glorious military history of the country. In addition to the Hussars Way, there was Cuirassiers Way, Infantry Square, Dragoon Path, General Street, etc. And as new streets were constantly being built, in order to keep the style, they had to resort to names like Sergeant Way, Bayonet Square, and Orderly Street.

A distance away from the house on Hussars Way, Krag and Keller got out of the car and walked the last part of the way. It was at the hour on a Saturday when people go to work. The sidewalk was crowded with workers, clerks, and shopgirls, everywhere the eager warning calls of the bicycle bells rang out, and the trams drove past, ringing, in their turn, and full of crowds. It was the overture to the mighty musical of the working day, this lively and rousing prelude of life that marks the dawn in all big cities.

"Look," cried Keller, taking his friend by the arm. They had stopped in front of number 28, on the other side of the street. Number 28 was, like most houses, a small, friendly family home with a fenced garden in front of it. On the path that separated the house from the street, among the blossoming apple trees, walked a young couple. The man was not actually in working clothes, but also not dressed in business clothes. One might believe that he was a busy shopkeeper or the like. The woman cheerfully carried a little girl in her arms. A shimmer of happiness spread from them and you could see from a distance what they were: a happy, young couple, a woman accompanying her husband on his way to work. The man said goodbye to his wife, stroked the little girl's hair and looked around for the tram, which approached the station with a screaming sound.

"This is our man," said Krag, stepping across the street, "unfortunately we must disturb the idyll." Keller followed him.

Every time Krag arrived to arrest a criminal, he paid close attention to how the person behaved the moment he realized that the police were there. In these fateful seconds, Krag could read much in the man's eyes—fright, confusion, desperation—and he had learned to distinguish between the helplessness of someone who doesn't understand and the helplessness of someone who knows he has been caught.

But when he stood in front of this young man and said, "We are from the police," he was not able to discover any of these telltale signs in the man's eyes.

"Your name is Singer?" Krag asked.

"Yes," answered the man, "Arnold Singer is my name. What do you want from me?"

"You are a laborer?"

"Yes."

"Maybe he's older than he looks," Krag thought. His face was neither regular nor pretty. But the eyes were uncommonly blue and open, fixed and calm, almost introspective. At this look, Krag involuntarily started, and now he saw that the eyes gave the face a look of unusual mental acuity. It was not for the first time that the detective was taken aback when he faced a man eye-to-eye and received a convincing expression of his intelligence.

This expression had nothing to do with the education or erudition of the individual; it was something primordial, something superior, energetic, and elastic, radiating from the searching look of the eyes. Krag had seen such eyes in parliament as well as in front of the railing at the court, both among famous statesmen and clever criminals from the depths of the Krydder District. Chance knows no rules, and at the same time Krag understood that the man he had in front of him would not be easily taken in.

While Asbjörn Krag made these lightning-fast observations, Keller had pulled out the photograph. They didn't need to make any comparisons, because the detectives had already recognized the young woman from the other side of the street. The laborer readily acknowledged that it was his wife.

"Yes. That's her," he said, taking her by her arm.

She had become a little frightened, which neither of the detectives found surprising. The word "police" always intimidates simple natures.

"But who owns the photograph," said Keller.

"Me. I probably lost it yesterday."

"Where?"

The laborer looked from one detective to the other. "Did he laugh?" Krag thought.

"I cannot be sure of the place," answered the laborer. "You never can do that when you've lost something."

"Where are you going now?" asked Krag, "To work?"

"Yes."

"Where do you work?"

"Good question. I need to find work, first."

"So, you don't have a steady job. What is your field?"

"Actually, I'm a gardener. But I also do other work."

"When did you come home last night?"

"About nine o'clock."

"And then stayed home?"

"No, I left about eleven o'clock and came back an hour later."

"Where did you spend your time?"

Singer shrugged.

"I went for a walk," he answered.

18

Krag pointed to the house.

"Let's go inside," he said.

The laborer went ahead calmly, but hesitantly. The young woman walked behind. They came into a rather large living room, which was nicely and simply furnished. The windows were open, the white linen curtains billowing in the morning breeze, it was a bright and friendly home. Krag noticed that a packed suitcase stood near the door. The woman brought the child into the next room, came back in, and closed the door behind her. Keller immediately started to examine the room, especially the carpet. The worker looked at him curiously. "Is he laughing again?" Krag thought.

Suddenly Keller turned to the woman.

"Was this rug swept today?" he asked.

"No, not yet," she answered timidly, as if the detective's comment contained a reproach against her skill as a housewife.

"Has it been swept since your husband came home from his walk last night?"

"No."

"It must not be either," said Keller, "the carpet must not be swept until I have examined it, do you understand?"

At the invitation of the laborer, Asbjörn Krag sat down, but the laborer himself remained standing. He waited.

"Dear Mr. Singer," said Asbjörn Krag, "you must tell us something about your evening walk."

"I'd like to know first," said Singer, "of what am I suspected? I suppose there is some unfortunate misunderstanding here. What is it about?"

"Robbery and murder," replied Krag. "Murder," he repeated clearly.

Strange. It was as if the room suddenly darkened, the white curtains seemed grayish, like the sheets on a deathbed, and in the silence that followed the words of the detective, a cold breeze blew across the room. In this way, the mind always feels the proximity of murder, it is as if the daylight turns gray with horror, when the most horrible of all words is merely uttered. Those present were also seized by a sudden and irresistible restlessness.

Krag interrupted the silence.

"Oh, you strong men and you weak women!" he said, "just look at your wife."

The young woman leaned over the table and clasped her hands against her chest. She was shaking, and her face was even paler than it had been before.

The laborer rushed to her and supported her.

"Clary," he said comfortingly, worried at the same time, "Clary . . ."

Then he looked at the police officers, looked from one to the other.

Asbjörn Krag noticed in his gaze both courage and anger.

Then he heard the laborer say to his wife, "Calm down, Clary, be quiet and rely on me."

At that moment a new man entered the room.

"Hello, Charlie," cried Keller loudly and happily, "is it really you, my old friend!"

V. The Wretch

The entrant, who came in suddenly from the adjoining room, didn't seem to be astonished at Detective Keller's greeting. He was a heavy-set young man, about twenty years old, dressed well, with curls that fell over his forehead. He looked as if he were a waiter or some subordinate office clerk; there was something childlike and insubstantial about him. It was not hard to pinpoint the similarity between him and Singer's wife, they were apparently siblings. The arrival of this man had come as a surprise to Krag and he was even more astonished that Keller knew the young man and received him in the same way that friends or police officers greet old acquaintances, which doesn't mean the same thing. It soon became apparent that the latter was true.

The appearance of the young man, however, caused the poor, unhappy Clary to further lose her composure. When her brother rushed into the room, she clapped her hands in horror.

"Wretch!" she cried, throwing herself across the table, hiding her tear-stained face in her arms. She cried softly. Her husband stood beside her and kept his hand on her shoulder.

Krag loved such dramatic scenes. For it happened that in moments when human passions erupted, more was revealed of the context of a conflict than in long and thorough interrogations.

The "wretch" remained silent, overwhelmed both by Detective Keller's presence and his recognition. For a moment it seemed as if he regretted that he had come in. He looked intently at the door and then at the window, as if estimating the possibilities of escape. And then he said, "I have nothing to do with this."

21

He reached into his pocket, drew out a bundle of bills, and threw them at the workman's feet, shouting, "Keep your money, I don't want to get caught up in your problems."

There was a scarlet flush across Singer's face.

"This isn't stolen," he said angrily. "It's my own money. And that's not how you treat money. Get out of here," he added threateningly.

Keller quietly whistled the chorus of the last popular operetta tune.

"What a comedy," he called, laughing and pointing his head at the "wretch," he added to Krag, who sat quietly by the window, following the course of events.

"This is Charlie Whist, he's a quick-witted kid, just a little soft of character. He was imprisoned for six months recently for ticket counterfeiting . . . And here you are again on the wrong track, friend, this time the crime is more serious. No, no, don't rely on escaping through the door. I stand between you and the door. And don't rely on the window, my colleague stands there. Let's talk to each other reasonably and reach some agreement. Stay calm. We don't need to shout so much that the whole neighborhood appears. What kind of money is it that you're throwing away so disdainfully?"

Charlie didn't answer. But Singer bent down and picked up the bills.

"It's my money," repeated Singer.

The little girl, left alone in the next room began to cry. Mrs. Singer rose, went in and came back with the child in her arms.

"I didn't ask you," began Keller again, "and please—call the nanny so that the child can leave, this isn't a child's business. But her mother has to stay, and everyone can stop thinking about the doors and windows. Nobody's going anywhere."

"We have no nanny," answered the young woman, "we are not rich."

"There is obviously enough money in the house," Keller said ironically. "As far as I can see from here, I estimate the money in your husband's hand to be a thousand kroner, which is a very nice sum, after all."

And turning to Charlie, "What do you know about this money?" he asked harshly.

And when Singer began to provide his answer, he shouted at him, "Shut up, man, you're a fool. If you prevent him from giving his own explanation, you are only making it worse for yourself."

"Shut up," muttered Singer, as if that address astonished him. Krag looked at him steadily all the time. This laborer had something both helpless and obstinate about him. Krag thought to himself that a wise man, caught in an extremely difficult situation and seeking time to find a way out, would act just like this. But there was something else about this man too, something that made Krag unsure; it was an expression of astonishment in his eyes, as if watching a spectacle that was none of his own making.

Charlie answered, "I got the money from him."

Krag watched everything down to the smallest details. "That one," said Charlie with a tone of contempt, meaning his brother-in-law. Charlie was a known criminal, yet it seemed as though he thought he was morally superior to Singer.

"When did you get the money?" Keller asked.

"Last night, I think it was between two and three o'clock."

"And you got the money from your brother-in-law when he returned from his nightly walk?"

"Yes."

"Did he go out to get the money?"

"Yes."

"Was it urgent?"

"Yes, because I was supposed to travel to South America by steamer at nine o'clock this morning. That's my suitcase, there."

"When did you get out of jail?"

"Yesterday afternoon."

"Well, I'm beginning to understand," Keller said. "They offered you a ticket to leave, and you wanted to go as soon as possible, because you didn't want to meet your old acquaintances after the counterfeit scandal. I see you nod, so it's true. And that's why you came to your sister for help. When?"

"Last night at eight o'clock. But he didn't come home until twelve o'clock. 'I'll get you the money,' he said, and left."

"Where did you get the money?" Keller asked, approaching the laborer.

"From a friend," replied Singer, "from a very good friend."

"That's nonsensical," Krag thought, "I would not have expected such a feeble explanation from of a man who looks so bright."

"What's the name of this friend and where does he live?"

"I can't tell you," replied Singer, "he doesn't want to be named."

Krag thought to himself, "He says it well, anyway. He speaks nonsense in a fairly credible way, maybe he believes he can deceive us by simulating stupidity. I suppose he is taking the following way out: he wants us to think that he is unusually simple-minded. But a sheep doesn't have such eyes; he belongs to the higher fauna."

Keller laughed loudly.

"These are schoolboy excuses," he said. "Dear Charlie," he went on, "prison seems to have been a good influence on you; at least it doesn't seem that you want to return there."

24

"I don't want to be involved in such things again," Charlie said gruffly. "I returned the money and want nothing more to do with it."

"You are right, my dear friend," replied Keller, patting the young man encouragingly. "This time you could easily have been involved in something way over your head. I can tell you that the money was stolen from Abbot Montrose last night."

"Abbot Montrose?" Singer said half to himself. "What?"

"Do you perhaps know him?" asked Keller.

"Yes," replied Singer.

"Did you work for him?"

"Yes, in his garden."

"Are you a gardener?"

"Yes."

Krag thought, "Now he doesn't answer haphazardly, he deliberately swims into my net. If you're being harassed, it's wiser to swim into the net than to avoid it, but he seems to know a way back out."

"When did you last work in his garden?" Keller asked.

"Yesterday. I probably lost the photograph there when I was weeding the flower beds."

"And you think the Abbot found it there and took it into his room?"

"I suppose."

Keller laughed loudly.

"Did you hear that, Krag?" he said, "He's going to have to do better than that. The whole thing seems clear to me. What do you think?"

"Almost too clear," said Krag.

25

Singer let his eyes rest first on Keller, then on Krag, and Krag thought, "He regards me with greater curiosity. It almost seems as if he has already seen through Keller. It's as if he wants to be clear about what danger I might pose to him."

Keller said, "We have nothing else to do here. Follow us, Singer."

"But I have nothing else to tell you."

Keller took the matter as settled, as if everything was already clear and done.

"Well," Keller said, "well, we want to get to know you a little better."

Suddenly Asbjörn Krag spoke, "You don't have blood on your suit?"

VI. Bright Colors

Asbjörn Krag's sudden remark was brutal, and he achieved his purpose. When she heard the word 'blood,' Singer's wife was terribly agitated again. Krag was not in doubt about her for a moment. Clary wasn't play acting, the fear that betrayed her feverish nervousness and radiated from her pale face was not contrived and calculating. It was equally certain that these two people, the gardener who called himself Singer, and the young woman with the child in her arms, loved each other. But where was the rock-solid trust with which a wife or lover meets the charges raised against the beloved? There was no trace of that here. Instead, she showed a marked unease, a lack of confidence that was conspicuous. It didn't take a lot of ingenuity to realize that something had happened in this young marriage that had undermined the woman's confidence in the man. All this Krag realized clearly, and he pondered how he could cause a new outburst in Clary.

"Arnold," Clary said, whispering uneasily, and joining the man with the child in her arms. He put his arm protectively around her waist. They formed a group that looked like the image of young married bliss if the environment had not been so unusual: the money that had been flung on the table, the young criminal, Charlie, poised in challenging defiance in the middle of the room and between him and the door Detective Keller with his pronounced police demeanor, watchful, hard-hearted, and casual—an official who can be seductively gentle with young women if he wants to know something from them; who jokes mercilessly when he arrests a bank fraud on the steamer bridge; who can push in doors with his round, good-natured shoulders; who responds to a heartbroken woman in tears with a smile and a snide remark.

27

The word 'blood' had been spoken, and it was as if the air froze in the room for a moment. In that silence, the whisper of the sympathetic young woman was heard as clearly as a prayer in a silent chapel. "Arnold," she said, "tell the truth, if you know something. Don't conceal anything."

"Oh, these women," thought Krag, "How often do they harm their husbands and their lovers!"

Her husband, however, took it with astonishing calm. There was nothing in his manner that showed anger that she had further distressed his situation through her distrust. He answered her only very seriously and urgently, "Trust me, Clary, do you understand? You cannot doubt me."

"No," she said, crying, "I don't want to doubt you."

"If she trusted him, she wouldn't cry," thought Krag.

Arnold Singer took a few steps forward.

"Who was murdered?" he asked.

Keller answered, "You are a hypocrite, my dear sir, just tell us the truth. Was Abbot Montrose murdered or abducted?"

"Abbot Montrose," murmured Arnold, "the good scholar Abbot Montrose . . ."

It seemed as though he was touched at the thought of the godly and mild prelate.

"Careful, Keller!" exclaimed Asbjörn Krag from his seat, "When someone uses that tone, he isn't harmless."

Keller grabbed Arnold's hands.

"There's no need for violence," said the laborer. "I'll go along quietly, and there's no blood on my suit."

Keller looked at Charlie.

"What do we want to do with this?" he asked thoughtfully.

"He should report to the police precinct," said Krag, "maybe we can use him."

That didn't please Charlie. He gave his brother-in-law a hate-filled look.

"You made a rod to beat me with," he said, threatening him with his fist. "I suspected something was wrong when you came home with all that money. If only I had just thrown it at your head."

Arnold was undisturbed. He only answered, "Prison seems to have made you cowardly and treacherous. Anyone might become that way in jail. Take me away, gentlemen."

Again, Krag wondered about his tone. He sounded more surprised and reproachful than actually agitated. It was as if Arnold were preoccupied with something, something he could not understand. And his tragic seriousness, which didn't agree with his youthful masculinity, was oppressive. The event seemed to have a terrible double meaning for him. At least that was how it appeared to Krag.

While he was led away, Clary's painful and desperate weeping echoed. Horror seemed to waft through the rooms, exchanging the friendly mood of the home for something unspeakably gloomy; when Arnold was led out, misfortune came in through the open door. Being unable to say something comforting to the young woman, Krag hurriedly left the room with the others—her lamentation seized his heart in an icy grip.

In the interrogation at the police station, which then followed, the impression was reinforced that Arnold Singer was intentionally engulfing himself in a mysterious darkness. He didn't bother with any details, only stayed with one of them: that he was a gardener and had spent the last few days working in Abbot Montrose's garden. His intentions were not difficult to see through. The only evidence of his involvement in the crime was the photograph that had been found in the mess left in the library and that was probably lost in the fight. If he succeeded in giving a credible reason for the presence of this

29

photograph in the library, he had prospects of removing suspicion from himself. If he could prove that he had really worked there, he would have gained much.

And Arnold Singer actually thought it possible that he could prove it.

He said, "I've been working in Abbot Montrose's garden for the last four days, and I was paid for my work last night by Abbot Montrose himself. I saw that the receipt for payment on a piece of paper that may still be in the library. It was thirty kroner."

On the other hand, he stubbornly refused to give details of where the thousand kroner he had given his brother-in-law during that night had come from.

The reason for his refusal was also easy to understand: he was stalling for time in the hope of finding a way out.

All this convinced Keller that Arnold Singer must be an unusually clever criminal. Asbjörn Krag didn't doubt the cunningness of the man either, but there was something in the laborer's superior demeanor that made him uncertain.

The day passed in looking for confirmation of the narrow explanations that had been given by Singer. In addition, Detective Keller had gone to the trouble of learning something about Singer's past.

Singer had also wrapped himself in mysterious darkness on this point. Fortunately, however, Keller was not relying solely on Singer. Above all, he could rely on the woman who was unable to hide anything in her misfortune. He also had brother-in-law Charlie, who was eager to lend a hand to the police because he was eager to convince them of his own innocence.

These inquiries brought some odd results for the zealous Keller. And while he was still busy, the newspapers published their stories. The newspapers described the impudence of the criminals. They "revealed" that the whole treasury had been looted and that a murderous robbery had taken place. All the newspapers agreed that Abbot Montrose had been murdered, and that his body had been taken away for some nefarious purpose, possibly involving black magic. The newspapers also agreed that the police must now cleanse the notorious Krydder District so that decent people could sleep safely in their beds. The stories all ended by saying that the investigation was being conducted by the well-known detective, Asbjörn Krag and his assistant.

That's how it stood when Krag and Keller met in the afternoon in the detectives' office.

Keller had found Abbot Montrose's note about the thirty kroner he had paid to Singer. So, until further notice, the details Singer provided were correct. "For the time being," Keller said, "we need to know more about one main character and two other people. I have already learned something about them. Look here, here I've recorded the matter. It's a strange story."

Keller had arranged the whole thing schematically. He read:

I. Arnold Singer, gardener.

II. Clary Whist-Singer, his wife.

III. Charlie Whist, his brother-in-law, recently released from prison.

Krag sat there playing with the scarf, which had been found in the looted library, the scarf in the "bright Spanish colors," in red and yellow.

"You can add another number," he said, "namely, IV. Hans Christian Andersen."

Keller remarked, "I think I've heard that name before."

"Very likely," replied Krag, "it is the name of the famous storyteller who wrote the tale of *The Ugly Duckling*."

VII. A Man

"But," the detective joked, "the famous storyteller cannot help bearing a name that has been very common in his native Denmark for two hundred years. You can be sure that a man named Hans Christian Andersen is at home on the friendly Danish shores."

Krag spread the Spanish scarf and let the colors glow in the sunshine that fell through the window.

"Anyway, it's the case with the owner of this scarf," he said, "with Hans Christian Andersen, the Danish sailor on the brig *Eddystone*. He's number four on our list."

"I have not encountered this name in the Montrose affair," said Keller. "Where the hell did you get that? Is that name on the hideous scarf?"

"No," answered Asbjörn Krag, "The scarf is printed: 'Cienfuegos, Bilbao.'"

"Maybe that's number four."

"Very funny. That's just the company name. It's embroidered here in the corner. Can you see Keller, the scarf is brand new and made of the best silk. One of the criminals lost it in the heat of the battle in the library. He probably just wore it once. It's a typical sailor's scarf, as they are sold in the Spanish ports in small seaside shops. There is no particular ingenuity in recognizing this as a clue. During the day, I made inquiries at the port and learned that the sailing ship *Eddystone* arrived from Bilbao, Spain five days ago and that one of the sailors had shore leave yesterday for the first time and went ashore with such a scarf. This sailor is a Dane named Hans Christian Andersen, which is the only thing he has in common with the author of *The Ugly Duckling*."

"Ah!" cried Keller, "that's very important information."

"Perhaps," murmured Krag, "but tell me more about Roman numerals I, II, and III."

Keller spread his papers and read:

I. Arnold Singer states that he is thirty-five years old and doesn't have a criminal record. Neither his fingerprints nor his photograph are in the police records. Claims to know nothing of the crime at the abbey. Gives remarkably sparse information about his life. Has learned gardening in the commercial gardens at Hobbemas in Amsterdam. Left Amsterdam when he was seventeen, later went to sea, and found work here and there. Asked if he worked as a decorator in the hotel, the Gilded Peacock, about three years ago, he admits this without further ado. (See II.) Indicates that he worked as a gardener in Abbot Montrose's garden last week and received thirty kroner for it. A note in the Abbott's hand confirms this claim. Explains that while working in the garden, he lost the photograph that was later found in the library. The photograph clearly shows fingerprints and traces of garden soil. These are Arnold Singer's fingerprints. (Keller's private note: The police must admit that the circumstances surrounding the photograph exonerate the laborer Arnold Singer.)

II. Clary Whist-Singer, daughter of the proprietor of the Gilded Peacock. She met Arnold Singer three years ago when he worked as a decorator at her father's hotel. Married him a month later. Explained that she loves her husband beyond measure, she further explained that her husband is a model of order and diligence. Every fortnight he gave her enough of his earnings to run the small household. He was at work most of the day, and often even at night, when he worked in remote places. Admitted that she sometimes wondered why Arnold didn't have a steady job. Also, admitted that she became restless when he would be gone for several days, and then she fancied that he had something mysterious about him; but as soon as he reappeared, this uneasiness vanished again. Twice she had happened to see him in possession of considerable sums of money, several large bills. But when she asked him about this money, he laughed and made excuses, saying that he had to get something for a friend. She had never seen this friend, Arnold didn't associate with anyone, and nobody came to their house. She confirmed in all respects the explanation her husband had given of the events of the night. She didn't believe that Arnold had come home later than two or half past two (the criminals left the garden at three o'clock), but she could not say with certainty. (Keller's private note: assuming that Arnold Singer is a criminal, the couple's married life is a typical picture of a criminal marriage. Arnold hasn't told his wife that they live on stolen goods. When he is away from home at night, which criminals must often be, he comes up with meaningless excuses. From this point of view, it is also quite natural that Arnold cannot tell his wife he has a steady job, otherwise she would easily catch him lying. Everything indicates that he wanted to conceal his crimes at all costs from his wife, whom he loves. He is the type of a modern criminal who leads a bright family life and a dark criminal life, one of those cunning cold-blooded individuals, who are a great danger to the state. With great skill he is now trying to save what can still be saved. He doesn't like that the careless Charlie is around. Charlie could easily endanger him, and if there were a way to get rid of him, he would take it. He undoubtedly committed the crime in the library in company with comrades. A very random trail has led the police to the idyllic villa.)

III. Charlie Whist, brother of II, son of the owner of the Gilded Peacock. An easy-to-see-through subject who plays a subordinate role. He was released from jail yesterday, where he had served his first sentence, and turned to his sister instead of the father, whom he dared not meet. When he received the travel money from Singer last night, he immediately suspected that a poor laborer could not easily lay his hands on such a large sum. And when the police showed up in the morning, he flung the money away because he didn't want to land himself in court once again. (Keller's private note: Charlie's account has been confirmed on a point-by-point basis by inquiries. He had taken a berth aboard the steamer *Argo*, which was due to leave for Argentina at 9:00 a.m. and events have forced him to postpone his trip.)"

"That's all," said Keller.

34

"It's not much, but I take it, on the basis of this cursory statement, it establishes Arnold Singer's participation in the crime. Now it is only necessary to get hold of his accomplices. And it almost seems as if you have already tracked down one. Tell me."

Krag had made no notes, but jokingly, he followed Keller's verbal protocol style.

He said, "Roman numeral IV, Hans Christian Andersen, ship's mate, on the *Eddystone*, owner of this scarf in bright Spanish colors, found in the library. Undoubtedly participated in the raid on Abbot Montrose's library. Got shore leave yesterday morning, didn't show up later on board. When the captain learned that the police wanted to get hold of Hans Christian, he replied that he, too, wanted to do so. It turns out that the sailor ensured that all of the captain's valuables took shore leave as well. In other words, he has run away, and must be sought anywhere other than aboard the *Eddystone*.

"Here, you can add," continued the detective, "as a private note from Krag: this escape proves that the crime in the Abbot's library had been planned for some time. The fact that this plan relies on a sailor aboard a ship that has just returned from a long journey makes it even more mysterious."

Keller let out a curse.

"To find a runaway sailor in the crowded harbor district," he said, "is like looking for a needle in a haystack."

Krag rocked back and forth in his chair, propping his legs on the table. He answered absently, as if his thoughts were somewhere else.

"It would never occur to me," he said, "to find a needle in a haystack. This eternal haystack is a bad example of the difficulties in an investigation. Anyone looking for a needle in a haystack must be crazy. So, the adage can only come from the deranged practices of a madman."

No one will ever hear what Keller would have replied to this remark for at that moment the door opened, and a man came in, tiptoeing like a thief. He looked around cautiously as if he believed himself to be followed and then carefully closed the door.

"Excuse me," the man whispered, "excuse me for coming here this way, but I'm afraid I might lose my job."

"I think he's crazy," Keller said.

"Maybe he came straight out of the haystack," Krag replied.

"I don't understand you, gentlemen," lisped the man, intimidated, "but I have something to tell you. I saw Abbot Montrose."

"You, and many others," answered Keller, "but since three o'clock this morning the Abbot has been missing."

The man answered, "But I saw Abbot Montrose at six o'clock this morning when he came back from a long journey."

VIII. The Gilded Peacock—I

"You're a waiter?" said Krag.

It was not hard to see, the black pants and the white, stained shirt betrayed him. Instead of a waiter's jacket he wore a large checked coat. He looked like an actor who might portray a waiter from a small tavern using his skills in costume and makeup. Everything about this man was weakened by nights with too much drink and not enough sleep. You could see pale skin through his thin yellow beard. The remnants of his hair were gracefully arranged with respectable economy and with the help of pomade, to conceal a waxing moon, if it is appropriate to venture an astronomical comparison with this decidedly-terrestrial skull. The look in his eyes was dull and murky, reminiscent of the greasy glow of a badly-washed shot glass. His nose was pointed and had the frozen look that characterized people who had worshiped Bacchus for a long time. He spoke in a low, confidential tone and bowed as if discreetly asking if he could bring the bill.

"Yes, I'm a waiter," he whispered, "and I'm very afraid that I might lose my job."

"What's your name?" Keller asked.

"Rudolf."

"And where are you a waiter?"

"I can only tell the gentlemen if you promise not to betray me."

"We promise that."

"When my boss learns that I've gone to the police . . . Oh my heavens, he's going to throw me into the street, head first."

"Is your boss so afraid of the police?"

"No, no, that's not what I meant, he just doesn't like the police mixing in his affairs. 'The police have no reason to interfere in a decent business,' my boss always says."

"He's right," said Keller, "and we don't want to embarrass you. So where are you employed?"

"At the hotel, the Gilded Peacock."

Neither of the two detectives betrayed by the slightest facial expression the surprise they felt. The small pause that followed the waiter's words, however, showed that they were both bemused by the unexpected coincidence that brought the threads of their investigation back to this hotel.

"And in this hotel, did you meet Abbot Montrose?"

"Yes."

"This morning at six o'clock?"

"Right after I got up, I always get up at six o'clock."

"Did you know Abbot Montrose before?"

"No."

"How did you know that it was him?"

"That's what I learned later—when I read the paper."

Keller scowled.

"Here we are," he murmured, "when a person disappears, and the newspapers sensationalize it, there are always a lot of people who want to fool us."

38

"Don't forget the Gilded Peacock," said Krag.

"That's true," Keller admitted. "We need to know more. Tell me, Mr. Rudolf, did you recognize the Abbot from the description of the newspapers?"

"Of course," answered Rudolf, "the priest's robe . . . the priest's robe with the rip in it."

"Hello," Krag said pleasantly. "Come closer and sit down . . ." And Krag pulled his feet off the table.

"The priest's robe," said both detectives, as if from one mouth, "was the Abbot wearing his vestments?"

"Not when he arrived," replied Rudolf, "but he had it with him. He came from the station with a brown satchel. I let him in, as the innkeeper wasn't up yet."

"Wait a minute," interrupted Keller. "Have you seen this man before?"

"No, never."

"Good, go on."

"He asked if he could get a room, because he wanted to rest for a few hours. He said he was returning from a long journey. I assigned a room to him and he went straight to bed after telling me to wake him at two o'clock. He wrote his name in the book, 'Thomas Uri, Shipbroker.' A strange name, don't you think, gentlemen?"

"A well-dressed man?" Keller asked.

"A very fine gentleman, a very decent tipper, a distinguished and priestly manner. Unfortunately, I didn't ask for his blessing when he left, for I had no idea who he was at the time, as I rarely have the opportunity to go to church," Rudolf lisped incoherently.

"What made you realize that it was Abbot Montrose?" asked Keller.

39

"I'll tell you in a moment," answered Rudolf. "At two o'clock I woke the gentleman. 'Has anyone asked for me?' was the first thing he said. 'No, Mr. Thomas Uri,' I answered, because if you remember the name of the guests immediately, you will always be treated well. 'I am expecting a gentleman,' he said, 'lead him up here when he arrives.' Barely five minutes later, this gentleman appeared. He was an older, very distinguished-looking gentleman, with a delicate, rosy skin and a soft beard. If I think about it, he may have been a bishop, but I've never been lucky enough to see a bishop. But that's how I imagined him, with a face that radiated peace. Well, this gentleman, whom I allow myself to call a bishop, though perhaps he was just a lender from the harbor area, I led this gentleman up to Mr. Thomas Uri, and they talked very quietly for half an hour, in Mr. Uri's room."

"Did you attend this conversation?" asked Keller.

"No, no, and it was so quiet that even just outside the room I could not understand anything they said. After half an hour had passed, Mr. Uri rang and paid his bill and then the two gentlemen went down together. Mr. Uri carried his little brown satchel himself, I was not allowed to. On this occasion I learned that Mr. Uri must have stayed in the hotel earlier, though not while I'd been working there. Because he was familiar with the layout of the hotel. He went straight through the door to the café, although the actual exit from the hotel leads through the vestibule and the doorway. Both Mr. Uri and the bishop stopped in front of the café bar to greet the innkeeper."

"Mr. Whist?" asked Keller.

"Yes, Whist, though this name is better suited to a young man than to the innkeeper, who is a dreadfully fat, heavy-handed man, all red and white, for he always stands behind the counter in a white suit with a white cap on his head. Mr. Uri knew the innkeeper, but he didn't speak to him, for the innkeeper seldom speaks, speaking bothers him too much, but they shook hands over the bar counter. I know this type of greeting, it means 'confidential friendship,' a grunt means 'recognition,' a little cough means 'welcome.' When Whist steps out from behind the counter, white and red like a threatening raincloud at dawn and raises his foot, then it means, 'Farewell, miserable gentlemen, get out of my house,' and it means, 'What shall poor Rudolf do?' So, you'll understand what I'm risking, gentlemen, and you have to be very careful and not betray me."

Krag tossed Rudolf a bill.

"Go on," he said impatiently.

Rudolf pocketed the money with an agility only possessed by those for whom the gesture is an old habit they have forgotten to change.

"I went to Mr. Uri's room," Rudolf went on, "which I always do to see if the travelers have forgotten anything. People are so forgetful. If the guests have forgotten something valuable, I keep it — uh, until they come back and ask for it, of course. I am, mind you, an honest person. If it is a little less valuable, I run after the guests and then always get a small tip. So, I opened the door and looked around the room. Nobody knows how to look around a room in a single moment like I do, gentlemen. I don't miss the smallest change. I saw immediately that the tip of a black piece of clothing was sticking out of the radiator grille. The radiator sits under the window and is covered by a pretty brass grille. Only my practiced eye could have discovered the little bit of cloth. I open the grille (it can be opened) and I pull out, what do you think? A priest's robe, Abbot Montrose's priest's robe."

"How did you know it was Abbot Montrose's robe?"

"Gentlemen," answered Rudolf. "I had read about the tattered robe in the paper, and that cloth was as torn as the papers had described. Then I thought to myself, 'Oh my God, the missing Abbot has been here,' and then I stuffed the robe back behind the radiator.

"I have not told any living soul of this. I knew that Mr. Uri knew the landlord, and I am too clever to betray the secrets of the hotel, and I am wise enough to understand that such secrets are valuable."

He patted his pocket comfortably, where Krag's bill was stuck.

Krag got up.

41

"When do you have to be back at the hotel?" He asked.

"At seven o'clock."

"Good. At seven-thirty, two gentlemen will arrive at your hotel."

"I understand, I understand," answered Rudolf. "But who will the two gentlemen be? The Gilded Peacock is a special kind of hotel and unusual guests attract attention."

"You're right," replied Krag, "who shall we be?"

"Forgive me," replied Rudolf, "but you must be a trapeze artist and the gentleman there a ballad singer. That's our hotel."

IX. The Gilded Peacock—II

"Ballad singer!" cried Keller.

"Trapeze artist!" Krag said, and they both laughed.

"Gentlemen, you should see our list of guests," said Rudolf eagerly. "It's a very special crowd that stops by at the Gilded Peacock." Since the hotel is located near the port, it happens that this or that sailor stays with us, otherwise the guests are almost exclusively performers. Simpson, the contortionist, or Miss Rosa, the lion-tamer, cause no more sensation at the Gilded Peacock than a merchant in the Palace Hotel. You should just hear the orders, 'One coffee for the lion tamer.' 'For the fire eater at table six, an ice-cold beer.' Yes, yes, that's the way it is with us. But there are also fine guests. Counts and all . . . It's a very good hotel."

"But ballad singer," muttered Keller indignantly.

Rudolf scrutinized the detective.

"Then maybe we'd rather say impresario with a specialty in boxing. We currently have no boxers in the hotel, so that fits well. At half past seven I will expect the gentlemen, I'll be in the café. Don't forget, gentlemen, don't come in through the gate, but through the café. Above the door is painted a peacock's tail. Bringing some light luggage is required."

After he had received repeated assurances from the detectives of absolute secrecy, Rudolf withdrew himself, bowing.

"What do you think?" asked Keller.

"I believe he spoke the truth," replied Krag, who had become very serious. "And I think it's Abbot Montrose's robe behind the heater. It doesn't look good for the dear Abbot. I'm afraid he's not alive anymore. But if he's been murdered, one of his killers was staying in the Gilded Peacock this morning."

"It's striking," said Keller, "that Arnold Singer is also connected to this hotel. I believe we are closer to solving the riddle than we suspect."

"The truth will come out," replied Krag.

The Gilded Peacock was in the Krydder District, but not in the worst part of it. Keller knew it by reputation and told Krag about it as they drove there in the car, each carrying a suitcase.

It was, as Rudolf had rightly described, an artist's hotel. Several times it had been under police surveillance. The one time involved gambling, the other time a young gentleman from the best society had disappeared into the cracks of the hotel, pursuing a pretty tightrope walker. The owner, however, had always managed to redeem himself. The hotel was on the police list, albeit not with a star, and first among the decent smaller hotels. It was known that the artists and Bohemians occasionally went there in the evening. The Peacock was also known for its exquisite cuisine, which catered to the tastes of an international and artistic clientele. Here, the Italian could get his garlic and macaroni, the French his "escargot," the German his sauerkraut, and the Russian his vodka. Chinese magicians ate roasted pork with chopsticks in a room of their own.

A cheap but tasty goulash was also served for conductors of Negro orchestras, but only for conductors, the colored musicians had no access to the restaurant.

It was already dusk when the detectives' car stopped in front of the small hotel. The street was narrow and twisted, and the tall houses that crowded together on either side of the road rose like steep walls around a gap. Over the gap hung the mist-gray evening sky, in which a pale, lonely star shimmered. It was an unusually beautiful and warm evening. The dimness of the street, the lights that were lit here and there in the

44

houses, transformed the insensate objects that shone in the dwindling daylight: the fantastic outlines of the signs, the bare brass basins of the barbers, the arched portals of the cinemas; the footsteps of the crowds on the sidewalks, which sounded like distant rain—the buzzing of voices, the droning of the cars, the ringing of the bicycle bells; and the indescribable smell of old stone houses and numerous old clothing dealers—all this gathered to create the vivid impression of the manifold life of the city, an impression that is otherwise only brought home by traveling from distant lands.

The detectives paid for the car, sent it away, and looked around. From the outside, the hotel looked very simple. It had a narrow façade, suggesting it might be of considerable depth. Above the gate hung a sign, "Hotel" and above the cafe entrance, a sign, "Restaurant." A small staircase with a brass balustrade led to the latter. Above the door was a gilded peacock's tail, only the tail, the bird already seemed to be on its way through the wall. In this way, on the threshold, the detectives received their first impression of this strange hotel, which they hoped would bring clarity to muddied waters.

First, the detectives entered a small, square anteroom divided by curtains that dropped down in heavy folds from brass bars. "Oh, those coffee-shop curtains," Krag thought with a faint shudder, "those eternal coffee-shop curtains that, like blotting-paper, attract all kinds of smells: of cigarettes, liqueurs, of indomitable idleness." The two detectives pushed the curtains aside and stepped into the café.

It was more bar than café. But right and left doors led to other dining rooms. Behind the bar sat the white and red Raincloud. Their observations were interrupted when a man approached them and reached for their bags. It was Rudolf.

"Gentlemen, do you want rooms," he asked, "big or small, single or double?"

"Two big single rooms," Keller answered. "Bring up our luggage, please, we want to have a drink."

"Very well."

45

Rudolf turned with the bags in his hand to the Raincloud, from whose reddish abyss now came sounds more akin to animal grunts than to human speech. Rudolf translated, "Room 6 and Room 8, gentlemen," and disappeared whistling softly with the bags.

Krag remembered that Room 6 had been Thomas Uri's room.

Apart from the typical stools in front of the bar, there were also small tables beside comfortable leather armchairs. The two detectives sat down at one of those tables, and a serving youth in a white apron, his arm full of bottles, approached. His cheeks were yellowish-white, and his lips were fire-red, and he laughingly asked with almost vicious childishness, "A little liquor, gentlemen, yellow, brown, or green?"

Without displaying too much curiosity, the detectives used the time to look around.

Behind the bar, flanking the Raincloud like friendlier and lighter clouds, sat four ladies. They were young and beautiful, their thick make-up could not hide their youth, nor their beauty. It seemed as though their lips and cheeks and eyebrows had been painted uniquely to match the colorful display of liquors that formed the background. The scene, with its oddly shaped bottles, in which, as in a prism, all the colors of the rainbow broke and multiplied in the magic depths of the mirror behind the bar, was completely overwhelming. On the top shelf stood the most remarkable bottles, and all the glory was crowned by a pear-shaped bottle of absinthe, the profound and poisonous-green contents of which would drive even the most degenerate alcoholics into raptures of delight.

The beautiful ladies behind the bar seemed, for some reason, to be engaged in handicrafts. One crocheted lace, her white ball had rolled over the counter and swayed on the white string like a dinghy on the sparkling glass surface. In front of her, on a stool, sat a very young man in a tailcoat, dull, with a glass of liqueur in front of him, not bigger than a thimble. He embodied the image of spurned love, while the deeply lowered eyelids of his beloved expressed heartless rejection. The unfortunate young man seemed fascinated by the dark depths of his glass and he held a cane with a silver handle under his left knee. His right leg sagged limply from the stool, over the open stocking at his ankle flashed a gold chain.

The other ladies were also diligently engaged in needlework, porcelain, or miniature painting—all the occupations of a distinguished home were abundantly represented behind this bar—and across the bar, an altogether less domesticated lifestyle gathered in the form of men chatting quietly or silently looming over the counter to cool themselves in the pleasurable unapproachability of the beautiful women.

In the midst of this flower bed, however, the redoubtable owner himself was enthroned in front of a silver champagne bucket surrounded by glasses. As he stood there, rosy red and white, he seemed to be a perverse butcher's fantasy; all that was missing was an apple in his mouth to embody a delicate pig's head. Quiet conversations in various languages drifted in from the other dining rooms, while guests were constantly going back and forth. A Chinese man, dressed after the latest European men's fashion, stepped carelessly and yet as cautiously as if he were ice skating. A Jew from the distant Crimea glided past on soft cat feet. Near the detectives, a middle-aged man was sitting alone at a table, staring hopelessly. His face was a striking prison-pale color.

Then Rudolf came to lead the gentlemen to their rooms—Thomas Uri's room.

X. The Singing Priest

It didn't cause a stir when the gentlemen left the bar of the Gilded Peacock. It seemed to be a rule that everyone did what he liked without others taking notice.

The colossal innkeeper behind the bar seemed to be fully engrossed in the cleaning of the champagne bucket—and nothing disturbed the four beautiful women from their domestic pursuits. One of them had started to polish her nails with a nail brush, and her friend beside her looked on with interest. Soon evening would arrive, the empty stools in front of the bar would fill, and a change in the employment of the ladies would occur.

The man with the prison-pale face stared blankly and indifferently through the bar as Krag and Keller walked past him.

Keller whispered, "I mean, I've seen that face, I just don't know where."

"Maybe in prison," said Krag.

"Prison Face certainly looks like he's come from there," Keller admitted, "but I'm sure there's another connection to his face. He sat there so strikingly limp, his eyes were so absent, it was as if he was listening with every nerve. But if I know him, he knows me too. This means we are no longer anonymous in this strange hotel."

Rudolf walked ahead with flying coattails, swinging his napkin back and forth. The whole time he murmured in a half-singing tone, "Gentlemen, this way, this way, gentlemen."

A signpost in the Gilded Peacock would have been helpful. Krag's assumption that a rather deep building hid behind the simple and narrow façade was true.

Apparently, the hotel had grown several times. The floors were stacked, like boxes messily glued together. The various builders, who at different times had enlarged this building, had taken no account of form or proportion; where they found space, they built a quadrangle and connected it to the old building with cleverly laid-out staircases and angular corridors. Corridors and stairs ran like mole's paths across the whole building. Down three flights of stairs and then down a section of corridor, up four flights of stairs, a narrow corridor with a sharp bend, then three staircases, and again a corridor dividing into several corridors, and again narrow corridors and new stairs.

From time to time the footsteps of the three men called forth a faint, metallic ringing sound that betrayed that the corridor was over a passageway below. The corridors, however, were covered with rugs that muffled their steps. On the wall panels between the doors, all in a red hue reminiscent of old blood, were painted fantastic animals, many of which belonged to some unreal world. A basilisk showed its terrifying eyes, a sea serpent snaked dangerously around the door jambs, and huge fairytale birds spread their wings far above the ceiling. Two kinds of animals, however, kept returning: a peacock, with its graceful splendor expressing indescribable well-being, and a monkey dangling from its tail, showing a grim but human face.

To make the confusion even greater, the doors had no sequential numbers, but the numbers were arranged according to a particular, and yet incomprehensible, system. So, for example, Room 6 stood beside Room 17 and Room 244 beside Room 88. However, Krag realized that there were systems when seeing that in one corridor the numbers 3 were collected in the following order: 3, 13, 23, 33, 43, and so on. In another corridor the numbers ran 2, 4, 8, 16, 32, 64, etc.

All this seemed calculated to make a strange impression. The most puzzling, almost eerie quality, however, was the silence in the hotel. That is, it was not quite quiet, but all the sounds were muted, as if they were coming through a thick fog. And in this hotel, there were many different kinds of sounds. Somewhere a monotonous voice sang a melancholy song, the singing came from very far away, and yet the detectives, as they listened, swore that it came from Room 33 near them; in this way, every sound was muffled by carpets and felt-covered doors. Mandolin playing was heard from another direction, the occasional echo of laughter arose from time to time, but it was impossible to tell where it came from. Some people floated past, waiters with wine in buckets, and guests, usually foreigners. In one corridor the detectives met an entire artistic family who seemed to be on their way to the circus, for they all wore black coats over their colorful fluttering costumes. At the head went the man, huge in girth but spry in step; his wife followed him, by no means as voluminous but still lumbering in her walk; then the other members of the family, down to a very small boy. One of the children whirled high in the air and came down laughing. Everyone crept almost silently over the soft carpet and disappeared in the depths of the corridor.

"Room 6, gentlemen."

Rudolf opened a door.

On the threshold Krag asked, "Can you find your way back, Keller?"

"No doubt," answered Keller, "I have an excellent sense of direction in the fog, we've gone west the whole time. So, the retreat must be steered eastward."

"Room 8 is next door," said Rudolf.

Krag wanted to head straight for the grille in front of the heater, but Rudolf stood in his way. He put two registration forms on the table.

"Your names, gentlemen," he said.

Krag took the pencil. What should he write? He looked questioningly at Rudolf.

Rudolf laughed happily. The waiter apparently had imagination. The names he suggested proved that he could be an author of adventure novels.

Bowing slightly to Krag, he said, "I feel as if this gentleman should be called Havana Jack. Occupation: trapeze artist."

Krag wrote without objection.

"And me?" asked Keller.

Rudolf considered.

"This gentleman is an impresario, specialty boxing," he mumbled. "We have to find something romantic. I enjoy having unusual names in the books. Oh, gentlemen, the other day a traveler named Raynor Schein arrived. I was happy all day! I suggest: Adam Zapel, impresario. Satisfied?"

"You are a master," said Keller, writing.

Rudolf took the registration forms.

"I will carry Mr. Zapel's travel bag to Room 8 now," Rudolf said, "to which I have the honor of welcoming him. I am sensitivity itself, and besides, I am afraid of the Raincloud. But if the trapeze artist from Havana wants tropical warmth in this room, the central heating is over there. (He pointed to the brass grille under the window.) What else would be in this room I forget. Forget me as well, gentlemen, until it comes to tipping. Good luck."

Then he disappeared with an elegant bow. A minute later Krag had opened the grille. He pulled out a black, crushed bundle of fabric and unwrapped it. It was a priest's robe.

He held the robe up to the light.

Near the hem was a tear that matched the tattered rag that the guards had found on Abbot Montrose's garden railing.

"There is no doubt," said Keller, "we are on the right track, this is Abbot Montrose's robe, and feel here, Krag, and here, and here—"

Krag ran his hand over the crumpled garment.

"Still wet spots, and red spots—that's blood, my friend."

"Undoubtedly," replied Krag. "The fate of the good Abbot worries me," he added seriously and thoughtfully.

"What do you mean?"

"I'm afraid he's no longer alive."

"Those bastards," cried the blunt Keller fiercely. "All traces lead to this strange hotel. The suspect, Arnold Singer, was employed here. His wife, that hypocritical little creature, is the Raincloud's daughter. And now we find this blood-stained robe here in the Raincloud's hotel."

He thought about it.

"I suppose we could take the hotel by surprise with fifteen men," he said after a while, "catching them in their own rat hole, the Raincloud and Thomas Uri and Prison Face and the trapeze artist and the boxer and the whole gang."

"First," replied Krag sharply, "I must protest most emphatically that Clary Singer is not a hypocrite. You are very energetic and efficient, Keller, but you lack patience and knowledge of human nature, and without these two qualities you cannot get to the bottom of this strange affair. Second, what do you hope to achieve by storming this hotel? We only know this one entrance."

"Isn't that enough for a raid?"

"Yes, for getting in, but you can be sure the hotel has several exits."

Suddenly the door was thrown open and Rudolf showed himself again.

"Hello," called Krag, and looked at the waiter with interest, "finally a human expression in this comedian's face. He is amazed. What has happened?"

"The Abbot," stammered Rudolf, "Abbot Montrose is here."

"Do you mean Mr. Thomas Uri?"

"No, not him, but the Abbot himself. He is singing."

"He's singing?" Krag asked.

"Yes," replied Rudolf, "he is singing. Many guests do this here at the hotel."

XI. Scholarship and Cocktails

Keller grabbed Rudolf's vest so hard that the unfortunate waiter swayed like a drunk.

"Listen, my dear sir," he said, "not only does the hotel seem insane, but so do the servants. Or are you drunk? What are you saying?"

"The Abbot," stammered Rudolf in alarm, "I assure you, gentlemen, the Abbot in person."

"Is singing." Said Keller.

"Yes."

"In the hotel."

Krag showed him the torn and bloody priest's robe.

"Put it away!" shouted the waiter, "put it back behind the heater, bear in mind when the Sinking Sun comes!" (Rudolf alternately called his boss the Raincloud, the Storm, and the Sinking Sun—aside from many other, less printable, names.) "By the way," he added, somewhat more confidently, "he won't come up here because he can't squeeze through the corridor . . . Ow!"

It was Keller who pinched his arm.

"That's right," said Krag. "Squeeze this fidgety waiter hard so we can squeeze something out of him."

Turning to the waiter, he continued, "You just told us that the man who left this suit here—that the man who called himself Thomas Uri was the Abbot. And now you offer us another Thomas Uri."

"No, no," stammered the waiter. "Mr. Thomas Uri was not the Abbot. This is the right one."

"But you don't know him. How can you claim it with such certainty?"

"Because he said so himself," answered Rudolf.

"Where is he?"

"He is in Room 333, it's right next door."

"Yes, of course," exclaimed Keller bitterly, "since this is Room 6, Room 333 must, of course, be right next door, a damned comfortable hotel, honored sir. How did he get here?"

"I have no idea. Suddenly, he was sitting in his room ordering a cocktail, a Morning Glory Fizz, to be precise. He is in full regalia with a gold chain on his chest."

"Cocktails," murmured Krag in surprise.

"Abbot Montrose," said Keller, no less astonished, "the scholar Abbot Montrose in this place, singing, and with a Morning Glory . . . I really don't understand—"

"You forget," said Krag, "that we have two alternatives, both of which are equally puzzling: either Abbot Montrose has been murdered by the burglars, in this alternative it is incomprehensible why they would take his body with them; or he has been kidnapped alive, this alternative is just as incomprehensible. How would the kidnapping have taken place? To some extent he must have been willing to go with them. How else would it have been possible for the robbers to carry him over the garden fence? So, let us not be too surprised if the matter takes an unexpected turn. There are certainly enough surprises waiting for us. I suppose the Abbot will have no objection," he said to Rudolf, "if we pay him our respects."

The waiter was sweating with fear.

"How can I get out of this jam," he said, "I'll be struck by a terrible thunderbolt from the Raincloud. Wouldn't it be better if I brought the Abbot here?"

"Why would that be better?"

"The Abbot has expressly forbidden all visits to his room. But he did expect that someone in this hotel would be asking for him. Well, I could pretend that I knew no better than that you were that someone."

Krag and Keller looked at each other. Keller was dissatisfied, but Asbjörn Krag said, "Do as you say, but go quickly."

When Rudolf was outside, Krag stuffed the tattered priest's robe back behind the radiator grille. Keller paced restlessly up and down the room.

"Do you really think," he said, "that this new figure, who has suddenly appeared, is the missing Abbot?"

"Nothing is impossible in our line of work," Krag replied. "We must expect this tragedy to gradually become a farce."

"Perhaps the famous Abbot has read so many scholarly works that he is no longer quite right in his head," said Keller, "I've heard that can happen. Maybe there is no break-in, maybe the Abbot himself, made insane through studying, has set this whole comedy into action. When madness takes possession of such learned masters, it is horribly jumbling to their unnaturally inflated minds."

Krag pointed to the radiator. "And where do you want to place Thomas Uri in that comedy with the torn, bloodstained priest's robe?"

"No, no, but—"

"And how are you going to explain Arnold Singer's money and the photograph?"

"Of course, but—"

"So far you have fought like a lion for the suspicion that Arnold Singer is a criminal, because it has suited your theories, but no sooner do you have new information, then poor Arnold Singer's situation improves considerably. This is why it is not pleasant to fall into the clutches of the police; the fate of the poor suspects is mostly subject to the casual hypotheses of gentlemen detectives."

"You're joking, dear friend," replied Keller irritably. "But, it's not easy to see through this damned mess."

"And how are you going to explain the noise of the many voices in the library at night and the sound of the many fleeing feet on the lawn that the policemen heard?"

Keller interrupted him with a wave of his hand.

56

"Quiet," he said, "the Abbot approaches."

Rudolf led the Abbot in but stopped himself in the doorway.

"Mr. Abbot," he said, "these two gentlemen ask you for the honor of a conversation."

He gently pushed the Abbot into the room and disappeared through the door. He was apparently afraid to get involved in the drama.

The Abbot remained standing somewhat uncertainly in the middle of the room. Was it really him? Neither Keller nor Krag knew Abbot Montrose by sight, and there were no pictures of him. But this man, who stood in front of them had a priestly appearance. His vestments were correct to the last detail, from the long ceremonial robe with the white collar, to the small square hat that the man wore on his head according to the custom of Catholic priests. There was also something priestly about his pale, clean-shaven face, which at the moment looked a bit exalted, and on his chest hung a thin, flashing gold chain.

Asbjörn Krag had immediately realized that when he came in, the Abbot was amazed to see the people he was facing.

"So, he was expecting to find people he'd met before," Krag thought, "and wonders how and why he is dealing with two others."

Krag pushed a chair over to the Abbot and asked him to sit down.

The Abbot sat down hesitantly.

Krag had set the chair in such a way that the light fell fully on the Abbot's face. Krag studied this face closely for almost a minute. Keller, too, said nothing; in serious diplomatic situations he always left the initiative to Krag. Keller had nerves of gutta-percha, no one could sit as completely unaffected as he, twisting his mustache and waiting. It was enough for him to see an almost imperceptible smirk around Asbjörn Krag's lips, and he waited for everything else quietly. Strangely enough, the embarrassing silence didn't seem to affect the Abbot in the slightest.

Suddenly Krag said, "After what has happened, we are delighted to see you again, Abbot."

The Abbot bowed his head with dignity.

"It is fortunate that such a distinguished representative of science has once again made himself known."

The Abbot bowed his head again, if possible in an even more dignified manner.

"Do you want whiskey or a cocktail?"

Keller could barely keep himself from laughing.

The Abbot, on the other hand, seemed to want to leave the choice to Asbjörn Krag, for he only once again bowed his head.

Krag rang the bell and gave his order to Rudolf. Keller opened his eyes wide on hearing the order, but Rudolf seemed satisfied that the company was getting on so well.

"Yes," replied Krag (although it was Saturday), "it is Thursday evening, ten o'clock."

The Abbot's eyes narrowed as if he was thinking deeply, the Thursday affair seemed to mean an unusually serious problem for him. Thereupon, he very slowly and clearly uttered a Latin phrase meaning, "Whom God gives children, he gives worries too." Then he sighed deeply.

Suddenly he looked up and seemed puzzled by the company he was in.

Keller whispered to Krag softly, "I think I'm right, it's a typical case of scholarly madness."

Aloud he asked, "Isn't it difficult to be so scholarly?"

The Abbot fixed his eyes on him but said nothing.

"I mean," Keller went on, a bit confused, "when you're educated so well, it's all up here in your head . . . I mean . . ."

The Abbot turned away from him, as if in the high regions where he lived he didn't grasp what this everyday man meant, but he bowed formally toward where Krag was sitting. His train of thought seemed only now to arrive at the same station where the detectives had alighted several minutes earlier.

"Thank you, a cocktail, please." he said.

With oddly perfect timing, from the door, a loud clinking noise could now be heard.

XII. Prison Face

It was the waiter who brought the drinks. There were different kinds of bottles and glasses, ice and cocktail shakers. Krag prepared the drinks like a trained bartender. The Abbot sat motionless and watched. Only the clink of the glasses could be heard in the room. But when the mixture was ready, a sigh sounded. It was the Abbot. But it was a sigh of relief, and the Abbot grabbed the glass.

He didn't take the time to toast with the others but emptied his glass in one go. It seemed to be a very fine cocktail, because his face suddenly brightened, and a captivating smile played around his mouth.

"You are a master," he said to Krag. "What's your business?"

"I am a doctor," replied the detective, "and the gentleman there is my assistant."

Keller fumed silently.

"Ah, and I believe you are also a master pharmacist."

The glass was filled anew, and he brought it to his lips.

It was as if his dormant vital energies returned with the help of this potion, or as if he had returned to earthly mundanity from those inscrutable heights where his soul otherwise hovered.

"What do you want from me?" he asked.

"My job as a doctor explains everything," said Krag. "As you can imagine, your disappearance has caused a great stir."

The Abbot became thoughtful again.

"Am I missing?" he asked, startled.

"Yes," replied Krag. "You mysteriously disappeared at three o'clock Friday morning. At the same time, your home was broken into and your entire library was looted."

The Abbot frowned.

"That's a God dam lie!" he shouted.

Keller became attentive. This distinguished and solid detective had never had a chance to be in the company of the higher priesthood, so he didn't know their customs. Yet he had a faint idea that the language the Abbot was using was quite unusual for those circles, as well as his in-depth understanding of cocktails. Krag, however, was not in the least upset by the Abbot's exclamation. Keller found that, at that moment, his colleague was acting like a doctor, an interested and patient doctor, examining a difficult patient.

Krag said, "And yet, what I said is true. I have connections with the police, and I know from a reliable source that the police are of the opinion that Abbot Montrose—that you—have been murdered."

"Ha!" shouted the Abbot and drank, "by whom," he added, looking sternly at the detective.

"No one, of course," answered the detective, with a firm gesture, "of course not, since you're alive. I'm only saying it to show you how thoroughly the police can be wrong. The police are facing a strange case here, and they don't have a clue what to do. This peculiar case, however, doesn't astonish me as a physician and psychiatrist. In my practice, I have seen several similar cases. Dear Abbot, the result of your extensive scientific work shows that your life has been filled with intense spirituality. As a result, your brain has gradually entered a high-tensioned state and, like a machine whose powers are exploited to the utmost, it is in danger of blowing up. A shocking event has given rise to a coincidental collapse, not a break, but only a temporary disturbance. The devastating event was the break-in to your library, you received a nervous shock, Abbot, and from that moment, let me express it this way, you lost the balance of your mental state."

The Abbot listened to Asbjörn Krag's statement with an almost fanatical interest, clearly showing that his brain was working strenuously to keep his mind focused. He stared at the detective all the time, blinking his eyes.

Then he pointed his index finger to his chest and said, "Me, I'm Abbot Montrose."

"No one doubts that," replied Krag lightly. "In general, no one who sees your truly priestly face, your pure noble features, can doubt that you were destined for science and the priesthood from birth."

"Is that really my friend Krag," Keller thought, "expressing himself in such trite sentences like a young girl who reads bad novels?"

The Abbot, however, was delighted with Krag's words. He expressed his delight by getting up slowly, striking a priestly pose, and gazing raptly at an imaginary gathering. Immediately after, he sagged and began blinking his eyes again, as if trying to capture a vision that has just departed. Then he dropped heavily on the chair and said, overwhelmed:

"Death and the Devil!"

Then he held out his hand to the detective, who pressed it warmly for a long time.

"And should anyone," said Krag, "dare to doubt that you really are Abbot Montrose—I mean, doubt it now, while your equilibrium is disturbed, surely you have evidence in hand that you are the aristocratic and noble scholar you claim to be."

Keller began to understand where Krag was going. And he listened to his strange dialogue with more interest.

The Abbot felt on his chest for a small medallion fastened to the thin gold chain that glinted on the black cloth.

He showed Krag the medallion.

The letters AM were engraved on the medallion.

"Armand Montrose," the Abbot whispered mysteriously, "that's me."

Krag opened the medallion. It was empty.

The Abbot nodded.

"As you can see, it's empty," he whispered, as if that fact contained valuable information. "But I have other things," he added, "I know where everything is."

"Where what is?"

The Abbot's answer revealed that there are certain words that a man not in possession of his spiritual equilibrium would be better to avoid. He said:

"The cospence."

But as he himself realized that this word lacked a certain *je ne sais quoi*, he repeated slowly, with emphasis on each syllable, like a man who is cautiously descending a staircase for the first time after breaking his leg.

"The correspondence."

"Aha, you have letters. Can I see them?" said Krag, holding out his hand.

The Abbot rose.

"Not here," he said, "I'll get them, they're in Room 333—"

As he pronounced the number, it seemed to contain at least three millions and several hundreds of thousands.

"I'll accompany you," said Krag.

But then the Abbot made a defensive gesture with his hand. He didn't want that. He would be back soon, though. The room was only three doors away from here, only three doors. He disappeared.

When the two detectives were alone, Krag bowed his head and laughed.

"Do you think he will find his way back?" Keller asked.

Krag listened at the open doorway.

"I can hear he's reached his room now," he said, "but it'll be a while until he finds the letters."

"What did you mean, that his soul is out of balance?" asked Keller. "I think that's a very mild expression."

"Too mild," replied Krag. "He's just drunk, totally drunk."

Keller shook his head doubtfully.

"A strange Abbot," he said, "a very strange man of God."

"Did you call him Abbot?" Krag asked, laughing again.

"Wasn't he Abbot Montrose?"

"No, certainly not."

"The hell! Who is he?"

"We'll find out soon enough," said Krag, and opened the door completely. "By the way, he's been away a long time, we'd better go to see him."

The moment the two detectives stepped out the door, a man passed them in the corridor.

It was Prison Face.

He walked across the rug with that peculiar, orderly, shuffling gait that marks convicts who have been long in prison, whose only exercise has been walking in the prison yard and pacing back and forth in their narrow cells.

But the carpet muffled his footsteps, and his sudden appearance, his pale face with cold, introverted eyes, made such an eerie impression that Keller could not suppress a "Huh!"

That's what the man heard. He turned and looked at them. The unusual paleness of his face seemed to broaden its dimensions, so that it seemed unnaturally large in the dark corridor. He didn't say anything, just looked at them and walked on in the same shuffling way until he disappeared into the darkness of the corridor.

His appearance had not only left an impression of horror, but also of danger. The two police officers rushed to Room 333 and knocked. When there was no answer, they forced open the door. Inside, the Abbot was sitting dead in a chair.

XIII. Room 333

The dead man sat in an armchair, as if he had sat down to rest for a moment. But there was a look of terror on his face. The priest's hat had fallen from his head and lay on the ground. The white collar was wrinkled and torn, one sign that an act of violence had been committed. Out of a wound in his chest blood ran down over his vestments. From the expression on the Abbot's face, which was distorted as if in a convulsion, Krag saw immediately that death had already occurred. He said, "The stabbing killed him instantly."

Keller pointed to the dead man's head with its dark, graying hair.

"He was not a priest," he said.

"No, no more than you or me," said Krag, leaning over the murdered man.

Krag was very serious and his voice shook as if a great misfortune had happened.

"It is very regrettable," he said, "that we let him go, but who could have guessed that a murderer was waiting for him. Nevertheless, I feel responsible."

"Yes," muttered Keller, as guilty as his colleague, "I feel the responsibility too. Murder is a serious thing. Maybe we could have prevented it with a bit more caution."

"Maybe," Krag admitted. "But as far as moral responsibility is concerned, I don't want to overstate it. It may be that the man sitting here was as guilty as the one who killed him . . . But what does he have in his hand?"

66

A piece of paper peeked out between the dead man's fingers.

Asbjörn Krag carefully removed it, smoothed it out, and read in a whisper something that seemed to amaze him in the highest degree.

Then he gave Keller the piece of paper and said, "Here's another connection to Arnold Singer. Do you recognize the handwriting?"

"It's Abbot Montrose's handwriting," replied Keller.

"His real handwriting, yes."

"But my God, that note is in police custody. That's the Abbot's receipt for his payment to Arnold Singer."

Keller read in a low voice what was written on the paper:

"Gardener S. paid thirty kroner for six working days."

"This is the same receipt," said Asbjörn Krag, "that our suspect, Arnold Singer refers to, as proof of his innocence. This piece of paper was in the hands of the police until a few hours ago."

"I locked it into the steel evidence locker in the detective's office myself, along with the other papers concerning the affair of the missing Abbot," said Keller, "and now we find it here in this hotel, in the hands of a dead man! Dear Krag, are we all bewitched? How did this piece of paper come to be taken from a locked compartment in the police station and arrive in the possession of this very intoxicated man? Why did he crumple it in his hand, as if life and death depended on its possession? Why was he murdered? And exactly who is this man, anyway?"

"And who is the murderer?" Krag added impatiently. "Tell me, dear friend, are you armed?"

"As always," Keller answered, pulling a revolver out of his pocket.

"I am thinking about the killer," Krag continued, "do you remember the man with the pale face, who appeared so eerily a moment ago?"

"You're right. No one else has been seen in the corridor, and the murder must have been committed within the past ten minutes."

Keller wanted to ring the front desk, but Krag stopped him, showing Keller how the bell apparatus that ran along the door frame had been cut.

"Ah," Keller said. "You rarely face such a deliberate murder. What do you think we should do now?"

"I suggest you stay here. You are armed. Besides, I don't think we have anything to worry about. Considering the dead man there, I believe that everything that was going to happen has already happened. Meanwhile, I will go down to the bar and alert the staff. I'll also summon some policemen from the street. The best thing is to close the hotel until further notice, it must be searched from the basement to the roof."

"Are you armed?" asked Keller.

"Yes," replied Krag. "I don't feel safe in the long corridor either. I advise you to lock the door when I'm gone. I'll give a clear signal when I return. In the meantime, you can search the room thoroughly, I am sure that there are several clues here. I'll put this piece of paper in my pocket until further notice. It will not be lost to the police a second time."

With that Krag went out; from outside he heard Keller closing the door. There was no one to be seen in the long corridor, and he heard nothing but the muffled sounds of a string quartet.

Krag realized that it was the music that had started down in the café, and he followed the direction of the sound. Doing so was necessary to find the way they had come—up and down stairs, to the right and to the left, as in a labyrinth; nevertheless, he began to find his way. He walked almost silently on the thick carpets, along the half-dark narrow corridor with its fantastic and distorted decorations on the walls, with animal eyes and strange bird's wings with the knowledge that a murdered man sat in one of the rooms—all of this imposed a strange mood on Krag, a feeling of unreality and horror that was new to him.

He found Rudolf at the entrance to the café and took his arm.

"I'll not betray you," he said, "and you need not worry, but something unfortunate has happened in the hotel. The gentleman in Room 333 was murdered ten minutes ago."

"Oh, heavens, the Abbot."

"Don't be too theatrical," said Krag, "but follow me and help me."

Krag quickly entered the café, not like a person with a terrifying message, but like a man who suddenly shows up at a dangerous hour and rightly takes command. Everyone became immediately aware of him. There were more guests now, almost all the stools in front of the bar were occupied, the beauty sitting behind the left end of the bar had put aside her crochet and had condescended to drink a glass with her admirer, the young gentleman with the gold chain around his ankle. The Raincloud was busy mixing cocktails. Krag approached him.

"I'm a detective," he said, "this is my badge. A few minutes ago, a murder was committed in your hotel. The murdered man is still sitting in his chair in Room 333."

When the Raincloud got this message, he was holding a glass under the seltzer siphon. For a second, the seltzer water overflowed and foamed over the glass-covered counter, which caused almost as much fright for the four beautiful women in their costly dresses and their admirers as the news of the murder. The ladies jumped up from their chairs and the young gentleman with the gold chain slid down to earth. But the Raincloud hastily closed the siphon's tap, and Krag had to admit that it was the only sign that the owner showed of his bewilderment. He muttered something that Krag didn't understand, and when he asked, the Meat Hill repeated, though vaguely, "It's been fifteen years."

"No, it's just happened," replied Krag, "scarcely fifteen minutes ago."

"It's been fifteen years," repeated the innkeeper, "fifteen years since a murder was committed in my hotel. That's why I know how to act in such a situation."

It seemed like a lot of effort to say so much at once. He breathed heavily.

"Close the kitchen door," he snapped, fixing his hazy eyes on the trembling Rudolf, saying, "Hrumph!" like an elephant that has gone mad. Rudolf hurried through a door behind the huge buffet, and Krag heard him screaming and shouting that the kitchen door should be closed.

Krag didn't object to this measure, although he doubted its usefulness, for so much time had already passed that the murderer had long since left the hotel. It would take many people to search the establishment from the basement to the roof. That's why he opened the door to the street to call for help. The air in the bar had been stiflingly hot, saturated with the smell of wine and perfume, so he felt the air from outside fresh and damp. "Sour like the air in a churchyard," Krag thought, in a strange connection to the dead man. The cacophony of the street fell over him, and the dense traffic passed him in a proud, thunderous chorus. In the lamplight, between the teeming people, horses, and carriages shone a few police helmets. Krag put his police whistle to his mouth letting out a shrill call. There was movement in the crowd.

After instructing the approaching policemen to guard the doors, Krag hurried back to Room 333, followed by several officers.

When he reached the threshold of the room, Krag stood quietly, though he felt a great desire to give vent to his astonishment in a loud cry.

The room was empty. Neither the murdered man nor Keller were there.

From the very back of the corridor came a moan.

It was the Raincloud, the proprietor, trying to get through the hallway, with his immense body getting stuck again and again in the narrow corridor.

Krag made a hasty estimation. Not more than seven to eight minutes had passed since he had left Keller and the dead man in the room.

And now the room was empty.

Krag had no idea that at the same moment a drama was going on in a completely different place and that Detective Keller was the unfortunate protagonist.

XIV. The Royal Family

As the doorway filled with the astonished faces of the staff and guests, and the innkeeper in the background complained bitterly about the narrow corridor, Krag stopped for a moment to get his bearings. This was a murder, but the situation seemed almost strange to him, the change had taken place with such cinematic speed. Barely ten minutes ago, Keller had locked himself in the room to guard a dead man—and now both the detective and the dead man had disappeared. There was the chair, there the table, nothing had changed, everything was as before. A fight had not taken place. There were no signs of violence. Nothing was broken. Krag stood silently, looking at the walls for a way out of his helplessness, but for his comfort he could find nothing but a portrait of the country's royal family, a portrait he'd also noticed, when he was last in this room with Keller and the dead man.

In the meantime, the innkeeper had succeeded in pushing himself through the narrow corridor – how he would get out again was anyone's guess. He shoveled the other curious onlookers aside, filling the door with his red and white mass and the silence with his audible breathing. When he spoke, he uttered the words asthmatically, his voice rattling as if from a sluice weighed down by its inner moisture.

"Where is the unfortunate man?" he asked.

"He sat there in the chair," replied Krag, "but now he's gone. One of my living friends was with him, but he's gone too—they're both gone. So you tell me."

"Are you sure it was in this room?" asked the Raincloud.

"Yes. I'm certain it was Room 333." Krag looked at the door to be sure. "Besides, I recognize the room, the chair, the table, the royal family, and everything."

"Was the door locked when you got here?" asked the innkeeper.

"No, it was open, but when I left my colleague, I clearly heard him lock the door from the inside. Nobody but Keller could have opened it . . . it's madness. I think the whole hotel is bewitched. You have a most curious hotel, honored sir."

"It is mine," gurgled the innkeeper, "and I may well arrange it as it pleases me. By the way, it's not out of the question for someone else to have opened the door from inside, honored sir."

"Who?"

"The gentleman you say was murdered."

Krag shook his head.

"You mean he was not murdered," said the detective, "that's impossible. The stab wound in his chest, the work of a long dagger, which had apparently passed through his heart, his extinguished eyes and stiff hands, which had already begun to cool. No, sir, such people do not stand up again."

Although he thought it pointless, Krag went to the corridor anyway and shouted Keller's name several times. His voice rang down the halls. But there was no answer. In fact, there was now nothing to hear in the whole hotel except the soft hiss of the central heating.

Krag returned to the room and sat down in the dead man's chair. He could not think of anything better to do. For the moment he was completely at a loss. He felt as if he had awakened from a dream and now was in a half-waking state where dream mingled with reality—as if the murder and the priest's robe and Keller and the whole mystery belonged to the dream, and the empty room and the amazed host belonged to this, by no means pleasant, reality.

But no, he knew that everything had happened. For the moment, however, the situation puzzled him. He was convinced that the puzzle must have a key and an explanation that must be tremendously simple, perhaps precisely because it seemed so mysterious. So, the dead man sat here, he thought, in this chair. Krag looked down at the ground. There was no trace of blood. He examined the rug more closely. No. Not the slightest trace of blood, really. But then he remembered that such deadly stab wounds through the heart left very little bleeding in their wake, often only a few drops on the white shirt.

The guests and staff outside in the corridor started whispering to each other now, and the moment started to seem ridiculous. Therefore, for solely selfish reasons, with regard to his own dignity, Krag made sure that the curious and unauthorized onlookers were sent away. As they walked away muttering, a waiter from the café pushed his way against the crowd to the innkeeper and whispered something to him. The innkeeper seemed surprised and immediately turned to Krag.

"He tells me," said the innkeeper, "that Room 333, this room, has not been occupied for several days. What do you say, sir? My ledgers are not lying. But here comes the porter, you can ask him yourself."

A man in livery, cap in hand, showed himself in

"Excellent," said Krag, "come in, you too, Rudolf—and shut the door. So now I am in the midst of people who will have something useful to say about this matter. This is a formal interrogation. Only a few minutes ago, I didn't think it possible that I would be sitting in the murdered man's chair asking people about the same dead man's whereabouts. He has disappeared, that's certain, both he and the detective. So—" Krag went on, speaking to the porter, "you say that this room has not been occupied for several days?"

The porter laid the hotel ledger on the table.

"Please, you can see for yourself," he said. "The room has been empty for the past three days."

"Good. But what do you say, Rudolf? Aren't you also sure that the man you called Abbot Montrose was in this room an hour ago?"

The name Abbot Montrose made a strong impression on those present. Of course, everyone had read the sensational articles in the papers.

The Raincloud made a heavy muttering sound.

"Yes," said Rudolf, "I am quite sure. He rang the bell and ordered a Morning Glory Fizz."

"The Crazy Professor's drink," muttered the innkeeper.

Krag didn't understand who he meant by 'the Crazy Professor,' and confined himself to keeping that name in his head for future use.

74

"Did you know then," Krag continued his interrogation, "did you know, Rudolf, that this man was staying in Room 333?"

"No."

"Is it possible that the man could have come into the hotel and gotten into this room without anyone seeing him?"

"That could be," answered the porter. "We don't always have the guests' comings and goings under control."

"And you served him the cocktails?"

The question was again addressed to Rudolf who replied, "Naturally. And he drank them right away."

"And you brought him on our request to Room 6."

"Yes."

"Oh, those damned numbers. Imagine, Room 6 being in the immediate vicinity of Room 333."

"It's my own hotel," growled the innkeeper. Krag interrupted him.

"And then?" he asked Rudolf.

"Then nothing happened until you came down and said that a man in 333 had been murdered."

Krag barely listened to what Rudolf answered. At last the detective seemed to have found a direction. It seemed to be in connection with the room, the astonished spectators in the room saw him glancing over the floor and heard him mumble, "No luggage . . . no luggage . . ."

"No, he didn't have any luggage," Rudolf said.

Whereupon Krag looked around the walls, his expression absentminded, mumbling to himself, "The royal family . . . the royal family . . ."

Suddenly he jumped up from the chair, flung open the door, leapt across the narrow corridor, and with a crash opened the door to the opposite room. He pointed in and shouted, "The royal family! Great God, the royal family!"

75

The royal family also hung on the wall in this room.

Then he ordered all those present out into the corridor, closed the door to Room 333 and showed them the number. Everyone stood and stared at the number dumbly with no idea what Krag meant. But Krag grabbed his head with his hands moaning, "Ah—Ah!" like someone who has made the stupidest of mistakes during a card game and discovered it himself.

Then he pointed to his own room, 6, and apparently calculated the distance between the two rooms 6 and 333. Then he pointed to the room next to Room 333, which bore the number 66 and asked, "Is this room occupied?"

"No," answered the porter, "this room is vacant too."

He tried to open the door to Room 66, but it was locked.

"Keller!" cried Krag, "Keller! Keller!"

No answer.

"Bring a crowbar!" he shouted, "and now!", a rising note of panic in his voice.

XV. The Explanation

After Krag pushed the now-broken door to Room 66 aside, he stopped on the threshold, surveying the situation in the room. He recognized immediately that the misfortune was not as great as he had feared.

Behind him, the owner, the police, and the waiters crowded.

Krag heard the innkeeper several times exclaiming, "That's the Crazy Professor, by my soul—that's the Crazy Professor."

"Oh, and now I recognize him too," whispered Rudolf, "without his hat he looks completely different."

The dead man was untouched. He was sitting in the armchair as he had been, and at his feet lay the square priest's hat.

And over on the bed lay Detective Keller.

It looked as though he had taken a nap and was angry now for having been disturbed.

He was lying on the bed dressed, the sheets pulled over his chin so that only his nose and eyes were visible.

But Keller's eyes said everything. They were sparkling with rage and bitterness. Krag had feared a catastrophe, but the expression in Keller's eyes was so unmistakably that of a living person, he immediately calmed.

"Why didn't you open the door?" Krag asked.

Keller didn't answer.

"Why didn't you answer when I called you? I shouted so loudly that even a deaf man had to hear it."

Still, Keller didn't answer.

"Aha," muttered Krag knowingly. He walked over to the bed and pulled back the sheets. There lay Keller, bound hand and foot, with a gag in his mouth. Krag undid the gag, and while he was still cutting Keller's bindings, his friend vented his anger with a volley of curses so inspired that Krag wished he were taking notes. No sooner was Keller free than he hurried to the window and continued his insults, which he seemed to address to invisible beings floating somewhere above the roof.

"Will you be done soon?" Krag asked.

"Yes, now I'm done," replied Keller, taking a deep breath.

He looked grimly at the Raincloud and provided him with some angry words about the hotel, which seemed to offend that mountain of flesh very much.

Meanwhile, Krag calmed his friend as best he could, sending the waiters away and keeping only the innkeeper. Krag had a certain confidence in the fat man.

"I was barely gone ten minutes," Krag said to Keller. "That's not very long, but you've done some extraordinary work in that time. I rarely have such luck."

He pointed to the dead man.

"Did he take you by surprise?"

"He's dead," answered Keller.

"Who could it have been? I myself heard you lock the door when I left you."

"Damn it, that was my bloody mistake. The bastards were already in here and I couldn't get out."

"Where were the scoundrels?" Krag asked.

Keller pushed aside a curtain. The curtain concealed a door that led to an adjoining room, but the door was so deeply set into the wall that there was enough space between it and the thick curtain for several people to stand.

"It happened when I locked the door, right after you left," Keller explained, "my back was to the curtain. Suddenly, I was being held from behind. You know how fast that goes, Krag. A minute later I lay bound on the bed, with a gag in my mouth, unable to move or scream. I had to lie still like a child in a cradle and watch as two men tossed the room searching for something."

"So, it was two men," said Krag, "and one was a sailor, wasn't he?"

Keller looked at him in astonishment.

"Did you see them?" he asked.

"No," replied Krag, "but only sailors can tie a rope in this way; I know this knot. Now tell me, how is it possible that you are now in Room 66 while I left you in Room 333?"

"This is Room 333," Keller answered.

"No," Krag said, showing him the number above the door.

Keller's astonishment was almost funny.

"I haven't been unconscious for a second," he said. "I can't explain that."

"Until a moment ago I thought it was inexplicable," Krag replied, pointing to the picture of the royal family on the wall. "This picture finally set me on the right track. Such a picture hangs in all the rooms, doesn't it?" he asked the proprietor.

"Yes," replied the innkeeper, "in most of them."

"And the room next door is furnished in exactly the same way as this one. As soon as I discovered that, I realized that we were wrong about the room number. The numbers were swapped while I was downstairs in the café."

"Impossible," roared the innkeeper, "this is Room 66 and has always been number 66, and the room we first entered is Room 333. I know my own hotel."

"Yes, of course. But as you also know, the number plates outside the doors are movable and can be changed. I don't understand why the poor man was murdered there. But that the unknown criminals planned the murder, that's certain, and they planned that the crime would take place in this room, so in Room 66. Keller might be able to explain why it would happen here."

Keller went to the open window and looked out.

"The cause may be," said Keller, "that this room has two exits."

"Two exits," muttered the innkeeper.

"Yes, one through the door and one through the window. Here, under this window, there's an iron fire escape ladder attached to the wall, I saw the criminals disappear through the window."

"Good," said Krag, "that's a decent explanation. For the rest, one can easily explain what has happened. The murderers wanted to lure their victim here. They swapped 66 with 333, while the unfortunate victim was with us. Then our drunken priest went astray, that's easy in this labyrinth, and the crime was committed. When we were in here, Keller, the murderers were already standing behind the curtain, listening to our conversation. They came out when I left the room. After they tied you up, they exchanged the numbers again. There you have the reason for all the confusion."

"That's how it must have been," said Keller. "Incidentally, I remember seeing one of the criminals open the door and do something. Immediately after the door was closed again, I heard your footsteps in the corridor, Krag. You must have just missed them. A rather thrilling thought, isn't it?"

"Strange," replied Krag, "while we were in the adjoining room, lost in consideration of why it was empty, the murderers were still here in this room. In truth, strange. Why didn't they flee through the window?"

"Because they wanted to seize the murdered man's letters, his correspondence, or 'cospence,' as he called it."

"The letters to prove he was who he claimed to be, Abbot Montrose."

"He's not Abbot Montrose," hissed the innkeeper, "he's the Crazy Professor."

"They took everything they found in his pockets," Keller went on, ignoring the owner's remark. "For a long time, they searched for a piece of paper, I suppose it was the receipt that you removed from the dead man's hand."

"The receipt that must have been stolen from the police archives," said Krag, "and which I now have it in my pocket."

"Yes. But when they didn't find it and heard you calling my name in the corridor, they gave up and hurried away. Oh, believe me, Krag, it was a joy to hear you shouting outside, and to lie here powerless with a gag in my mouth."

"We must move the murdered man," said Krag, "I'll call the officers . . . The peculiar thing about this investigation, Keller, is that more and more secrets are emerging the more we delve into them. It's as if, like the Hydra, with every lopped-off head so many new ones will grow in its place. Now, there are no fewer than eight questions to answer:

Where is Abbot Montrose?

Is he dead or alive?

How did this man come into possession of Abbot Montrose's papers?

Why was he murdered?

Who murdered him?

Where are the murderers?

Are these criminals the same ones who abducted and murdered Abbot Montrose?

Why did this man impersonate Abbot Montrose?"

"As far as who murdered him," answered Keller, "I can perhaps give you some information. One of the criminals was an unshaven man with a brutal face. As soon as I saw him, I thought of your storyteller, Hans Christian Andersen."

"Ah, the missing sailor—here again we have a connection with the drama in the Abbot's library."

"And as for where the murderers are," Keller went on, pointing to the window, "we at least know that the criminals are no longer in the hotel."

Krag went to the window. It led to a dark and narrow yard. He looked questioningly at the innkeeper.

"They have to pass through two yards before they get on the street," he explained. "Everything is nested in this neighborhood. Yes, yes, through two yards, only then do they get on the street."

"Which street?" asked Krag.

"Hussars Way," replied the innkeeper.

"The street where Arnold Singer lives," murmured Krag thoughtfully.

"That name again."

XVI. The Greengrocer

Asbjörn Krag became more and more convinced that the innkeeper of the Gilded Peacock was an innocent, as well as a particular type of urban character, a man who apparently had nothing directly to do with the uncanny events. However, the innkeeper was so closely connected with several key characters in the drama that the detective decided to keep an eye on him. So, he ordered the innkeeper to report to the police department the next morning. The innkeeper scolded the police for sticking their noses into his business and cursed loudly about the Crazy Professor as he returned to his peerless bar, where police officers kept watch over every door. Krag also sent the two waiters away.

When Krag and Keller were alone again with the dead man, Keller silently regarded the murdered man's face. Then he said, "I don't understand how we ever considered this man to be an outstanding priest. Just look at the features of the unfortunate fellow. Aren't they a striking image of a deteriorated alcoholic? Why did he have to be murdered?"

"He was a drunkard," said Krag, "and went around spouting stupidities. That may be enough explanation. Under the influence of his intoxication he was talkative. Other people would not have liked such a chatterer going around freely. Maybe he knew too much, yes, surely, he knew too much. That's why he had to be eliminated. Had we kept him with us for another hour, he might have given us the solution to the riddle. While we chatted nonsense with him in our room, the criminals were close by, probably listening to our conversation, a frightening thought. They realized that their own safety was in danger if the good professor was walking around freely and talking freely in his drunken state. They decided to get rid of him; they made a smart plan as quickly as I've ever seen. But the fact that they risked so much

83

convinces me again that this strange story contains a profound tragedy. I'm afraid, dear friend, that the real Abbot Montrose is no longer alive."

"I'm sure he's dead," Keller said, "but I can't see why these dangerous criminals chose Abbot Montrose as their victim. When criminals set to work, they prefer that other people be out of their way, and when they do seek out prey, they usually expect more than what they could expect from Abbot Montrose."

"Perhaps," Krag remarked thoughtfully, "the crime has grown like a rolling snowball. Initially, they may have planned only an ordinary nocturnal break-in at the Abbot's residence, knowing that the church funds, a few thousand kroner, were in his safe. They were, however, surprised by the Abbot. To save themselves they had to get him out of the way. Then they had to dispose of the Crazy Professor, because he put them in danger by revealing them in his drunken chatter."

Keller laughed.

"That sounds quite logical," he said, "but your explanation falters. Why didn't the criminals content themselves with killing the Abbot? Why did they carry him away with them? Or is it conceivable that the Abbot is alive, and that he climbed over his high garden gate like some sort of ecclesiastical monkey? In the company of the criminals? And why would such clever criminals, as they seem to be, take such a poor fool as the Crazy Professor to be their accomplice?"

"Riddles," Krag replied, looking again at the dead man searchingly.

He added, "This man might almost have given us the solution. His death prevented him from doing so. Nevertheless, I believe that his fate will help us. He lives nearby in the greengrocer, Mrs. Grossmann's, house, as Rudolf told me. Grocery stores close late today, we will certainly still meet Mrs. Grossmann. If we find out more about the life of this strange man, we will certainly learn more about the drama in which he played a part."

There were footsteps in the corridor, and a police officer came in and said that the patrons downstairs in the café were angry because they were being held in the bar. He asked for instruction.

"What shall we do with these people?" asked Keller. "We cannot arrest all of them after all, we have no right to do that."

He pointed to the window and continued, "The murderers, the only people we care about, have already disappeared on this path."

"And are now long gone," added Krag. "Open the doors, officer, and give the people in the café their freedom. Everyone is free to go."

"Maybe the innkeeper," said Keller questioningly.

But Krag replied, "A man of his size doesn't flee."

After he had given the policeman instructions about the dead man, he left the room together with Keller.

Down in the café, they took Rudolf with them so he could show them the way to the grocer, Mrs. Grossmann. As they passed, they saw that the bar was in a state of complete dissolution. The girls stood in an intimidated cluster behind the bar, the Raincloud sat motionless behind his shining mixer, so electrifying the air with curses that it was dangerous to come near him. And the whole motley swarm of foreigners, contortionists, trapeze artists, and lion tamers talked across each other. Cursing and swearing could be heard in all languages. Amid the confusion, however, two huge policemen stood immovable and incorruptible. When the order to open the doors came, they enforced it, violently flinging the doors wide. The sour, cool spring air streamed into the café, making the girls shiver. They began to sneeze and climbed onto their stools. Out on the sidewalk, one could see curious pale and staring human faces. Carried in by the breeze, the sounds of the street drifted intermittently into the enclosed, muggy café . . . Now, however, a strange thing happened: at the moment when the doors were opened, and the way was clear, nobody wanted to leave. Only a few older members of the bourgeois who had boldly come to this Bohemian hotel sneaked away. Then the Raincloud called, "Close the doors!"

The doors were closed, but not locked. The young gentleman with the golden chain at his ankle took his place on the stool in front of his beloved again. The guests gathered around the tables, because all felt the need to be together and to discuss what happened . . . But by then, Krag and Keller, led by the waiter Rudolf, had arrived at the greengrocer's as she was about to close her shop.

Mrs. Grossmann was a corpulent, self-assured matron, like one found in most grocery stores, where they stand behind the counter like old grenadiers with sashes crossed over their chests. She had a small mustache on her upper lip, and her hands were as red as ripe tomatoes. She looked at the two police officers with quiet curiosity, and looked at Rudolf, whom she apparently knew, with decided suspicion.

Rudolf explained to her that the two gentlemen had questions about the Crazy Professor.

"He lives with you, doesn't he, Mrs. Grossmann?"

"Yes," she answered carefully.

"The two gentlemen are from the police," Rudolf explained.

"As you say," she answered, not astonished.

Suddenly she fixed her angry eyes on Rudolf and shouted, "Get away, you miserable gnat. I want to talk to the police alone."

Rudolf disappeared quickly. When the two detectives were alone with the woman, Krag said, "You don't seem to be surprised that the police call on you about the Crazy Professor?"

"No," she answered.

"How long has he been staying with you?"

"Two years. At first, I always asked myself: Aren't the police coming for him soon? But no police came. After a while, I stopped asking myself. And now the police are here. No, it doesn't surprise me."

She reached for a large bunch of keys that hung on a rusty chain around her waist.

"I don't think he's home," she said.

"He's not at home," replied Krag. "But we want to see his room."

She lifted a hinged flap in the counter and the detectives stepped closer. First, she wiggled to the shop door and locked it. Then, the rattling bunch of keys in her tomato-red fist, she led the detectives through a room behind the shop, full of sacks and boxes and all sorts of fruits and vegetables. The air was thick and tangy. From this room a door led to a dark corridor. The damp had eaten through the walls. There was a smell of potatoes and cabbage and other vegetables in the dark corridor as well, and the odor accompanied them up the stairs until it was gradually replaced by a subtle, ineradicable smell that rises from old houses, and which originates in the damp walls and old rotten wood. The stairs were narrow and creaked miserably under the weight of the heavy woman. You could not see your hand in front of your eyes, but Mrs. Grossman walked through the darkness with practiced security and the detectives followed at her heels.

Finally, she stepped onto a landing and put the key in a door.

All the while she had not said a word, but now she asked, "Has he been arrested?"

"No," replied Krag. "He is dead."

For a moment everything was silent. The key chain hung noiselessly in her hand. There was no sound from outside either. The tight, oppressive darkness surrounded them. But from below a rough, sucking draft of air came up through the narrow staircase.

She turned the key in the lock, and the three people entered a dark room with only a single gray patch of light from the square, gray window, no larger than a stone tablet over a grave.

Keller breathed deeply.

"What a scent!" he exclaimed in astonishment. "Flowers . . ."

"Fresh flowers," said Krag, "like in a churchyard. Make some light."

XVII. The Keys

It took a while before Mrs. Grossman found the box of matches in her roomy bag. Meanwhile the two detectives waited in the darkness, breathing in the strange flowery scent that filled the room.

This fragrance gave those present a visionary sensation of the closeness of death. It was as if the Crazy Professor had arrived home before them, or as if his soul had been carried up the stairs by the damp, cold breeze in the old house, and enveloped the room in a scented harbinger of doom. In a similar fashion, living people often feel the closeness of the recently deceased in the churchyard or from the scent of the flowers on the coffin. The feeling of being close to something unusual became so strong in Asbjörn Krag that he repeated in a loud voice, "Make some light!"

At last the old woman managed to light a match. At the first flickering light, the detectives saw a jumble of colors in the room, an intense glow along the walls. When the lamp was burning, they understood the source of the patchwork of colors and the stunning floral scent: in a long line of bottles and jars stood all sorts of beautiful and strange flowers. Some were in bloom, but most—and these were the ones that gave off the most numbing scents—were already withering, hanging sadly and dying with drooping heads.

"Grave robber," Keller mumbled, critically examining some wilting tulips in a green bottle.

"Hardly," replied Krag, who had taken a hasty look at the unusual flowers, "these flowers are not torn from funeral wreaths or bouquets, they are cut from flower beds."

As he murmured the names of the various species, he shrugged as if pitying the fate of these beautiful flowers. He lifted a black liqueur bottle in which two charming sun roses stood and said, "These were picked in a hothouse barely twenty-four hours ago."

"But in which greenhouse?" asked Keller.

Krag answered indirectly, "Abbot Montrose was a great flower lover."

Keller laughed and pointed to the small room.

"Haven't you given up on the insane merging of Abbot Montrose and the Crazy Professor?" he sighed. "Just look at all those emptied and half-emptied bottles of brandy, and liqueurs of the most ordinary variety. Isn't that proof enough that whoever lived here was a committed – and indiscriminate – drinker? And the drunkard's madness has expressed itself in the fact that he decorated the empty bottles with beautiful flowers, like he was decorating corpses. There must have been a big funeral here recently, since he was totally drunk when we met him."

"He was almost always drunk," the grocer tossed in with her coarse bass.

Keller laughed, as only one who is completely convinced could laugh, "And if I think of the distinguished and respected Abbot Montrose, the famous scholar who spent all day in his library engaged in his studies, I am, unfortunately, unable to follow you in your, ah, bold speculations."

"I make no assumptions," said Asbjörn Krag, who still gave the flowers his undivided attention. "I'm certain of this, though: these flowers have not been stolen from a cemetery, they have recently been cut in a greenhouse. You know, dear friend, that Abbot Montrose was a great admirer of flowers, he had a beautiful hothouse in his garden. These flowers belong to Abbot Montrose—be he dead or alive."

"So, you still cannot separate yourself from the idea that the Crazy Professor is identical to Abbot Montrose?"

"Heaven forbid, I dropped that idea a long time ago. I only notice that these flowers bring us back to Abbot Montrose's garden, and thus to the criminal. I regret anew that our mad professor is dead, otherwise he could easily have helped us solve these riddles."

Mrs. Grossman grunted impatiently. Apparently, she didn't want to hold back the information she could give. Like most of her social class, she was happy to serve the police.

She said that the Crazy Professor, who called himself Warren Strantz, had rented this room two years ago. Right from the start she noticed that he behaved strangely.

"First, he apparently had nothing to do," she said, "and people who have nothing to do are always suspicious to me. In addition, he had this characteristic: he liked to disguise himself. When he came into possession of a professor's cap, like the ones worn in universities, he was very pleased. Then he walked around on the streets here in the neighborhood, talking to people until the police took away the professor's cap because he was always gathering a crowd and blocking traffic. He drank terribly, and when he was drunk he gave long, strange monologues up here in his room. He could preach for hours, as if he were standing in a pulpit. Often, he came home with flowers, which he hid under his coat, and as soon as he had finished a bottle he decorated it with flowers. Yesterday he was wild with joy because he had come into possession of a whole priest's vestment with which he had dressed himself."

"Did he ever have visitors?" Krag asked.

"Rarely," answered Mrs. Grossmann, "and then it was mostly drunkards that he had picked up from the street and with whom he was drinking. But a few hours ago, there were two men asking for him."

Krag asked her to describe these two men and Keller soon realized that they were the men who had gagged him, bound him, and then fled through the window. He told Krag this. Krag was not surprised. The detectives now began to examine the room, but they found nothing but a few well-worn garments and a few sheets of paper on which strange glyphs like crow's feet had been scratched.

"Are those Assyrian characters?" asked Keller, looking at the paper curiously.

Krag laughed.

"It's either the writing of a deranged man," he answered, "or a language that no one living can interpret. I believe the former, because these are fragments of esoteric knowledge. Here are some Chinese characters, here some hieroglyphics, here a Greek sentence. Hello, what is that?"

Krag had accidentally brushed his arm against an old jacket that hung in a corner and had heard a clinking sound.

The detective held the jacket up to the light. He saw that it had fresh traces of earth.

"Is that his jacket?" Krag asked.

Mrs. Grossmann nodded; the garment was well known to her.

Carefully, so that the earth would not crumble, Krag examined the jacket.

In the pockets were some ripped green leaves.

"He's been carrying flowers home in this jacket," Krag said, "just recently, because the pockets are still damp from the wet leaves, and there's fresh dirt on the fabric. You'll see it's dirt from Abbot Montrose's hothouse."

"But what is clinking in the left pocket?" Keller asked impatiently.

Krag carefully removed a key chain from the pocket. Mrs. Grossman stepped closer to see better.

"These are not his keys," she muttered.

"How do you know that?"

"What would he want with all these keys? He had only one key for the front door and one for his door. And they are not there."

The key ring contained fourteen larger and smaller keys, all steel, plain and finely made. Among them was a small silver key that evidently belonged to a shrine. And on the key ring was a silver tag hammered to look like a shield, where the letter M was engraved.

"I like these kinds of discoveries," Krag said cheerfully. "Let's see, what do we have all together now? Above all, the receipt for Arnold Singer's six days of work, then the scarf in the bright Spanish colors, and the photograph of Clary Singer, the jacket with the fresh dirt stains, and finally this key ring. While they are very different, such things eventually form a chain. The shield bears the letter M, as you can see. Montrose?" Krag asked thoughtfully.

"In that case, these would be Abbot Montrose's keys," said Keller, "and then what?"

"Yes, and then what?" replied Krag, weighing the key ring in his hand. He counted the keys.

"Fourteen," he said, "if they are Abbot Montrose's keys, we can go through his apartment and see where they fit."

"And how can that help us?" Asked Keller.

"No, of course," muttered Krag softly and absentmindedly. It was as if he was thinking out loud and didn't care about the others in the room. "But," he added, "if there are keys here that don't fit into any lock in the Abbot's apartment, two superfluous keys, two keys whose use is unclear to us—"

"What then?" Keller asked again.

"Yes, then what?" said Krag.

Then they heard noise on the stairs.

93

XVIII. Fate

Asbjörn Krag had told the officers to carry the dead man from the Gilded Peacock to his apartment. Now as the detectives heard footsteps on the stairs, they thought for a moment that it was policemen carrying his body.

Krag opened the door so that the light fell onto the dark stairwell. The sound of footsteps fell silent. Below stood a single uniformed officer.

"What do you want?" asked Krag, who didn't know him.

"I want to speak to one of the detectives, Mr. Krag or Mr. Keller."

"I'm Krag, what do you want?" Krag asked again.

"Come closer," he added.

The policeman climbed the creaking stairs a few steps and said, "I've already asked for you at the Gilded Peacock. There they told me that you were here. I bring you a message from the police department."

"Regarding the missing Abbot?" Krag asked.

"Yes."

"Did they find him?"

"No. But something else has happened. Arnold Singer, the suspect in custody, tried to escape."

Krag was startled. Keller, still in the room, had heard what was being said and was now hurrying to the stairs.

"But he was caught, if I understand you correctly?" asked the detective.

"Yes. He was caught—an hour after his escape. And now he is in custody again. In this case, however, the chief wishes that at least one of the detectives would come down to the police station. There's an automobile waiting downstairs."

Krag and Keller negotiated for a moment and agreed that Krag should go with the policeman, while Keller would remain to get more information, mainly about Arnold Singer, whom the owner of the Gilded Peacock must know better as his daughter was married to him.

Asbjörn Krag learned the details of the unsuccessful escape attempt while in the car. These circumstances greatly astonished him, completely changing the idea that he had formed of the peculiar prisoner. He had expected more from Singer. Krag found the escape attempt very foolish in itself, and being so awkwardly set in motion, the detective suddenly had the surprising idea that Arnold Singer had attempted escape solely to reinforce the suspicions that weighed against him.

At eight o'clock in the evening, Singer had petitioned to be questioned again. Not in one of the police interrogation rooms, but down in the detectives' offices. He had probably noticed at a previous interrogation that a door from the corridor led directly out onto the street, and that the circumstances favored an escape attempt. He had taken advantage of that. When the police guard led him down, he struck the officer with a heavy blow that stunned him for a moment, pushed the door open, and hurried out into the street.

Two circumstances occurred that prevented his escape. First, the blow he had given the guard had not been strong enough. The man yelled for help and police came rushing out of all the doors. The second, and worse circumstance, however, was that when Arnold Singer reached the street, he happened to meet a policeman who was heading inside. This policeman, whom the fugitive had almost knocked over, immediately grasped the situation and ran after him down the street. After these two came more policemen. They shouted, "Grab the thief!" and passersby began joining the pursuit. It became a typical city manhunt, up one street and down the next: Arnold Singer ran for his freedom like a hunted fox and the crowd followed him like a pack of baying hounds. Finally, Singer disappeared through an open doorway into a house where he succeeded for some time in escaping his pursuers. But the police surrounded the house on all sides. Whereupon they searched it from top to bottom. Arnold Singer was finally found in the basement and led back to jail in handcuffs.

That was the story of the strange escape in a nutshell. The policeman who told Krag about it had taken part in the chase himself.

Krag asked him how Singer behaved after his arrest.

"He laughed," replied the policeman. "He seemed to think it was a joke, and he was willingly lead off. He said that he was accustomed to a daily walk and that a little running had done him good. He had nothing else to say."

Although it was already eleven o'clock, Krag decided to visit the prisoner in his cell. Arnold Singer lay on his bunk when Krag entered. He didn't rise during their interview.

"You have made a great mistake with this escape attempt," said Krag, "and made your situation worse to a notable degree."

"As you say," answered the prisoner. "By the way, I thought you believed that nothing could make matters worse. As far as I remember, the police had evidence that I was Abbot Montrose's murderer."

"No proof," replied Krag sincerely, "but evidence so strong that your position is in great danger. At any rate, that was how your case looked this morning. However, the situation improved during the day. "

"How so?"

"We found a note from Abbot Montrose about paying you thirty kroner for six days of work."

This message didn't seem to make a special impression on Singer. However, he approached it logically, stating that, "The only thing the police have against me is a photograph found in the looted library that belongs to me. The police claim that I lost it before the murder or robbery. On the other hand, I say that I lost it while working in the garden. I think the police will lose their argument the moment I can prove that I really worked as a gardener for Abbot Montrose. And isn't this proved by the discovery of the receipt of wages?"

"Undoubtedly," replied Krag, "and that, as I have already said, leads to a considerable improvement in your situation. Later, however, two circumstances occurred that made it worse again. The receipt no longer exists, it was stolen from the police archive this afternoon."

This information seemed to make a very strong impression on Arnold Singer.

He rose to his elbow and stared wide-eyed at the detective.

"Stolen?" he exclaimed. "That little receipt, that unimportant piece of paper—was it really stolen?"

"Yes," replied Krag.

Then Singer erupted in a forced, cheerful laugh.

"You call it an unimportant piece of paper," said Krag. "But for you it had a sizeable importance."

"In other words," said Singer, "a person who understood the importance of this piece of paper has made it disappear."

"We can assume that."

"Maybe my life depends on it," said Singer, "so this person must be my enemy."

He stretched back onto the cot and put his arms behind his neck.

"I am not afraid of him," he said.

"You have no reason to be afraid," replied Krag, "we found the thief."

"So—oh, who is it?"

"Do you know the Crazy Professor?"

"That's not a name."

"His name is Strantz."

"Did the police find him?" Singer asked hastily.

"Then I regret, on behalf of the police," continued Singer, "that they failed again in an attempt to prove my guilt. I know Strantz. I worked with him in the Abbot's garden. Unfortunately, he was a bad gardener—he stole flowers."

"Strantz, too, cannot testify for you," replied the detective.

"Why not?"

"Because he's dead. At about eight o'clock this evening he was stabbed by an unknown murderer. You really have dangerous enemies, dear Mr. Singer. The only document that could prove your innocence was stolen, and the only person who could testify in your favor has been murdered."

After these words of the detective, Singer remained silent for a long time. Then he asked, "Had Strantz been interrogated?"

"No."

Again, there was a long pause, whereupon Singer said, half to himself, in a strangely disturbed voice that shook Krag, "That's fate."

XIX. The Figure in the Garden

Asbjörn Krag was unhappy. Even as circumstances more and more indicated that Arnold Singer was the criminal, he himself became more and more convinced that something was wrong. Krag was always inclined to doubt when others were convinced. For him, the deciding factor was this: the simple solution that Arnold Singer was the culprit seemed too simple in relation to the strange circumstances that surrounded the crime. First, the enigmatic fact that the Abbot had disappeared, dead or alive. Furthermore, that people who remained at large apparently risked so much to reinforce the suspicions that the police had against Singer.

Only when Krag imagined that those who were guilty were still running free, was the murder of the drunken professor comprehensible. For he alone could testify to the innocence of Arnold Singer. That's why he was removed. Dead men don't talk.

On the other hand, Asbjörn Krag had to admit that Arnold Singer appeared to be guilty. The self-assured, superior nature of the man had made a strong and somewhat positive impression on Krag, who involuntarily felt attracted to strong-minded people, whether they appeared in the guise of robbers or honorable men. It didn't quite make sense to him that this man should have played a subordinate role in the crime. Krag had thought him the leader of the gang from the start. Such a calm and determined man like Arnold Singer was born to command. The fact that he had been on the scene of the crime before could be proved almost irrefutably. Even his failed escape attempt spoke against him strongly, because an innocent man doesn't flee from jail, but stays and defends himself. So, if he was guilty, all the circumstances indicated that he was the ringleader. But how could it be explained that his accomplices didn't shy away from committing a

99

murder that would destroy the proof of his innocence? Why would they eliminate someone who could testify on Singer's behalf? Normally comrades, at least subordinates, tend to do anything to come to the aid of a leader who has gotten into a tight spot. Here again was a circumstance that lacked a logical connection.

And there were many such contradictions. That was what astonished Krag and caused him to study the details of the matter thoroughly. The main event itself had such a gap in its logical sequence. The raid on the abbey with the intention of robbing its coffers, was an everyday affair. In the midst of it, however, appeared one very pointless circumstance: the disappearance of the Abbot. If Arnold Singer was guilty, he had acted with great intelligence from the moment of his arrest and had carried out his defense with strict logic. But then there was his completely senseless escape attempt. What did that mean? Another thing: the crime was carried out with boldness and cold-bloodedness, but why had the criminals made that poor flea, the drunken, foolish, chattering Strantz, their co-conspirator? At some point, a devil always stuck his head out, both in terms of human behavior and in the evolution of events, upsetting everything. But where did this devil come from? All these contradictions aroused in Krag the idea that an even greater mystery was at play. Something was rotten in Norway.

The next day brought several unexpected events.

The police had good press that day, thanks to the arrest of Arnold Singer, which the newspapers described as good detective work. The journalists were of the universal opinion that he was probably the gang's criminal mastermind. Otherwise, the newspapers were full of editorial remarks about the private life of Abbot Montrose, on which, apparently, no shadow fell. They praised his scientific thoroughness, his charity, and his diligence, and regretted that such a rude fate had brought down so distinguished a scholar all too soon.

So far, only a few newspapers had mentioned the murder of Warren Strantz, the mad professor. The connection between this murder and the crime in Abbot Montrose's library was not quite understood. However, one of the newspapers reported that the murdered man had worked as a gardener in Abbot Montrose's garden, and commented poetically:

It's as if a mystical death is following the people who have witnessed the rush of spring in Abbot Montrose's garden this year. First the Abbot himself was attacked one night when the trees were covered with new green leaves. Then death sought out one of the workers, who had done his part to ready the garden for the arrival of the season. Will Death's scythe cut short even more such lives before the garden is in its full splendor?

Strangely enough, this poetic effusion bothered Asbjörn Krag as he entered the Abbot's garden through the wrought-iron gate that morning. Over the last few days, spring had made great progress there. The foliage had become denser and a lusher green, and a mild southern breeze slowly drifted through the trees, with that incomparable spring bravado that fills people's minds with yearning melancholy and makes them feel more intensely the narrowness and ruthlessness of life. Some mysterious reverberation lay in the familiar song of the season.

Krag thought about the man who had now disappeared, but who would otherwise have wandered among these same trees during the spring. It seemed to him that he heard a mystical reverberation himself, something of the soul of the riddle in the rustling of the treetops. It was as if a mysterious voice that had come from far away was caught here on its silent journey and received a resounding expression. The scent of the sprouting garden reminded him of the exaggerated and perverse floral splendor in the wretched room of the mad professor; and again, it was as if the scent of the flowers brought him closer to the merciless vision of the churchyard and death . . . He was alone in the garden and spring was spreading its dominion and abundance, from the deep black earth to the highest treetops.

When Asbjörn Krag approached the Abbot's rooms, he saw that everything was as it had been on Saturday morning when he had left the house. The battered window still hung crookedly on its rusty hinges, and down on the yellow earth, the shards of glass flashed like silver in the sun. Krag went through the wide front door and into the library, where everything was still untouched. He walked around the rooms and looked at the various objects that were related to the crime: the shattered cabinet, the overturned chairs, the broken inkwell, and all the little objects that had been thrown about during the fight. He also examined the traces of blood that were found here and there: on the carpet, on the desk and—with insidious clarity—on the white field of the door. Eventually, he stepped back and viewed everything at once. The room's disturbance revealed broken but violent activity. One thing he realized was that the fight that took place here had been a life-and-death struggle, chairs had served as weapons, ink flowed wildly, the numerous traces of blood indicated that knives had been used . . . But Krag mused, completing the train of thought—Arnold Singer's suit had no tears, no blood stains.

Then the detective moved on to the reason he had come. He examined all the locks and he realized immediately that his assumption regarding the keys he had found in the mad professor's room had been correct. It was Abbot Montrose's key ring. This circumstance confirmed the complicity of Strantz; he had probably taken the keys during the fight, or . . . and at that thought Krag shivered—or perhaps this key ring was among the objects that the kidnapped Abbot Montrose had been carrying.

Krag had soon found the key to the front door and found the keys to the other doors, the bookcase, desk, wardrobe, even the kitchen door, to the wine cellar, and to the greenhouse. But there were four keys left, the use of which he could not explain: a Yale key with the stamped number 22,470, an ordinary front door key, a locker key (or drawer key), and a small, artfully forged key whose peculiar shape suggested that it belonged to a precious and antique reliquary or strongbox.

Asbjörn Krag removed these four keys from the key ring, held them in his hand, and looked at them for a long time. They convinced him that there was a secret that was not limited to the ruined library and the lush spring garden alone. Krag had settled himself in the Abbot's armchair with the keys in his hand. From his seat he had a view of the garden and the wide gravel path, shaded by dense trees, leading to the hothouse, whose gleaming glass roof was visible among the trees. He felt the cold metal of the keys between his fingers and had a clear, instinctive feeling that they were the keys to more than just the locks they opened. If he could divine their purpose, he would get to the heart, to the solution of the mystery . . . He would come to a door, open the door with its key—and what would await him inside? A dead man? A dying man? A living man, a happy one? Again, it was the disappearance that bothered him, the unbearable questions: Why was the Abbot taken away? Why wasn't he here?

A faint sound from the garden reached his ear. He looked up.

Between the trees, a human form appeared, stepping out of the shadows.

The figure came closer.

It was a black-clad gentleman of priestly appearance, approaching the library, and stepping out of the shadows, standing on the yellowish soil in strong sunlight.

XX. The Letter

Asbjörn Krag remained immobile and watched the approaching man. In the large, silent garden the appearance of this man seemed like something unreal to him. Suddenly the figure stood there, sharply lit by the spring sunshine. When he had stepped out of the darkness, taking shape under the tangled shadows of the trees, in the strange state of mind in which Krag found himself, the sudden appearance of this man was like a revelation, a personification of the dark and the mysterious. When he saw the priestly character of the figure, an expectant shiver ran through Krag. His thoughts had been intensely concerned with the Abbot's disappearance; now he involuntarily sought a connection between the missing man and the gentleman, who, apparently familiar with the surroundings, bowed his head and walked thoughtfully on the golden shimmering path of the garden.

The stranger was about fifty years old. He wore a tall hat and a long frock coat that was buttoned up to the neck. A white scarf enhanced his priestly appearance. In his hand he held a cane. He walked along through the garden like a man who knows where he wants to go without deviating to the right or left. Krag noticed that he had come in through the south gate of the garden, which was rarely used and was always locked.

When the man reached the library, he stopped and looked around, scrutinizing. Krag could now see his face more closely; it had a sense of calm and kindness; white whiskers gave him a certain grandfatherly look.

The man walked slowly to the middle window and looked into the library, shading his eyes with his hand. It looked as if the great mess in the library startled him, for he withdrew with a violent gesture. But then his eyes fell on Asbjörn Krag, who was sitting in the armchair, and his face was immediately illuminated by joyful recognition, as if he had found the one he sought. He waved to the detective, who got up and opened the door.

The stranger came in and gently shook hands with the detective.

"I was hoping to find you," he said. "I recognize you because of the pictures in the papers."

He looked at Krag curiously.

"So, this is what a detective with an international reputation looks like," he mumbled.

Then he glanced around the room again and his voice trembled slightly as he continued, "The terrible condition of this room shocks me, in this place of peace. When I think of the glorious hours I spent in this room, if—"

"Why do you seek me? Why did you expect to find me in this place?" Krag asked. "And with whom do I have the honor to speak?"

The stranger searched for a business card in his wallet and answered, "I came looking for you here because I have an important message for you and because I didn't find you at the police station. Here is my card, my name may not be unknown to you."

Krag took the card which the gentleman handed to him and read:

Thomas Weide, Juris Doctor, attorney-at-law.

"Ah, the well-known jurist," said Krag, "I know you by name. I am pleased to make your personal acquaintance. Incidentally, when I saw you outside in the garden, I thought you were a clergyman."

Weide nodded, pleased. He seemed to take that remark as a compliment.

Krag picked up one of the overturned chairs and asked him to sit down.

"I suppose," he said, "that you come because of the sad business involving Abbot Montrose?"

"Quite right," answered Weide, "I'm Abbot Montrose's legal adviser and also his friend. I have always been interested in church matters and I like to associate with clergymen. Many members of my family belong to the religious class. All of this, of course, has had an effect on me, so that my nature took on something of the priestly. However, questions of conscience have brought with them a certainty that I could not follow the desire of my heart and become a member of the priesthood."

Krag stared in astonishment at this man, who had come to such an extraordinary place at such an extraordinary time to tell him about his private circumstances.

"I may say," Weide added, "that I'm the only one who has the confidence of Abbot Montrose's, yes, maybe I'm his only friend."

Krag noticed that this remark was in the present tense and he said, "If you've read the papers carefully, you realize that you can hardly say you *are* Abbot Montrose's friend."

"You think I *was*?" answered Weide.

"Yes," said Krag, "unfortunately there is much to suggest that the Abbot is no longer among the living."

Thomas Weide looked inquiringly at Krag through his gold-rimmed glasses.

At this, Krag hesitated. Weide's gaze was probing and careful.

"I dare say," said the lawyer, "that I still *have* the confidence of Abbot Montrose, in this matter."

The detective listened carefully.

"You express yourself with such determination," he said. "Do you know something?"

"Yes."

"Is Abbot Montrose alive?"

"Yes," answered Weide, "anyway, he was alive yesterday."

"The day after the robbery. Do you know his whereabouts?"

"No."

Krag got up and walked up and down the room a couple of times. Finally, he stopped in front of the lawyer.

"If you speak the truth," said Krag, "Abbot Montrose has laid a veil over a mystery, that veil places great obstacles in the way of the law-enforcement efforts to solve a crime. This crime already involves a murder. As a lawyer, you must know what that means. Why doesn't Abbot Montrose show himself?"

"He announced himself."

"Yes, as you suggested, why doesn't he appear in person?"

"I don't know," answered Weide, "I received a letter from him."

As the lawyer took a letter from his wallet, Krag could barely control his curiosity. Nonetheless, he did not fail to examine the envelope before he unfolded the letter. It was a simple gray-blue business envelope, but it was very crumpled and dirty, as if it had gone through many and not very clean hands.

The envelope had no postage stamp, but the postmark on the back showed that Weide had paid postage due, which the lawyer confirmed in answer to Krag's question.

Krag pulled the letter from the envelope and unfolded it. It was an ordinary square-lined stationary. It, too, was crumpled. Krag read in low tones:

Dear friend!

Tell the police that I live and have withdrawn from my job to spend some time quietly in special studies.

Your devoted friend

Montrose.

After Krag had read these few words carefully, he put the letter back in the envelope and asked, "May I keep the letter?"

"Yes," answered Weide, "I hardly think Montrose would object."

"Are you sure the letter was written by the Abbot himself?" asked the detective.

"There can be no doubt about that," answered Weide. "Abbot Montrose's handwriting is so unique that it is impossible to mistake it for another. What else do you think of the letter?"

"It has arrived so unexpectedly," said Krag, "that I have not yet had time to form an opinion about it. One thing is certain, however, that this letter doesn't simplify matters, but on the contrary, makes them much more mysterious. The letter reveals that Abbot Montrose was still alive yesterday, but it gives no information as to whether he is still alive today."

"Could it be possible?" murmured Weide uneasily. "Why do you think—"

"Because the letter proves," replied Krag, "that Abbot Montrose is no longer master of his actions. I hardly believe that I am mistaken if I dare to say that he is being held somewhere against his will."

While the detective was talking, he had been carefully studying the envelope.

"This envelope reveals many things," he said. "Would you like to know what it has told me—"

XXI. The Five Devils

Asbjörn Krag pushed his chair to the desk and put the envelope and letter in front of him. Thomas Weide, Juris Doctor, stepped closer, interested.

"Note that both letter and envelope are very wrinkled, and the envelope is very dirty. I assume, Mr. Weide, that the letter already looked like this, when it came into your possession?"

"You can assume that, of course," replied the well-groomed jurist, laughing. "I was very surprised when I received a letter in this condition and recognized Abbot Montrose's handwriting. One might think the letter was sent from a coal shop."

"Or was procured by a coal merchant," added Krag, "because the postal service doesn't treat letters this way. However, I put weight on the fact that the stationary itself isn't dirty. On the other hand, it is as wrinkled as the envelope. In other words, the letter was mauled before it was dropped in the mailbox. The letter was stamped by the C-4 post office, which means it was dropped into a mailbox in the center of the city and stamped at the post office at four o'clock yesterday afternoon. It is also stamped B-37."

"Very true," said Weide. "My office is in mail district B, and the letter was in my mail when I arrived at my office this morning."

"Another remarkable circumstance is," Krag went on, "that the letter is unstamped. If we associate this with the dirty envelope, etc., we come to the simple conclusion that the letter was dropped into the mailbox by a street urchin who kept the postage and sent the letter without it. In any case, there is one thing we can assume for certain:

Abbot Montrose did not himself send out an unstamped, dirty, wrinkled letter."

"Unthinkable, unthinkable," answered Weide, shaking his handsome head.

"On the other hand, it seems unthinkable to me that Abbot Montrose would entrust such an important letter to the hands of an urchin who would treat it like that. In general, the extraordinary importance of the letter must remain the decisive factor in our conclusions. I want to make the paradoxical statement that the letter is so important that it should not have been sent."

Weide laughed.

"What do you mean?" he asked.

"I mean, if Abbot Montrose is alive, it would be very important for him to let his friends and the police know. But this would most certainly happen if Montrose presented himself and said, 'Gentlemen, I am not dead, I am really alive.' Judging by the letter, he seems to be fully aware of the extraordinary sensation his disappearance has caused. However, much as he loves his undisturbed peace to work, he must understand that, for his own sake, by appearing, he would have eliminated the scandal that threatens his name. But he doesn't do that with this letter, which doesn't even reveal where he is. Is it like Abbot Montrose to behave this way? You know him, is this like him?"

"Not at all," answered Weide, "on the contrary, I know no one who treasures his reputation like my friend Montrose, no one who is more afraid of making a sensation and a stir. In a case like this, he would have hurried to the police himself."

"And since he hasn't done so," said Krag, "we can safely assume that my first assumption is correct, namely, that he cannot because he's not master of his actions—that, in other words, he's under the control of criminals who, for some reason, have threatened him into writing this letter. Let us suppose, moreover, that Abbot Montrose is held captive somewhere in the suburbs, or, more likely, a good distance outside the city. Then we also have an explanation for the spotty appearance of the

110

letter. Because in this case, one of the thieves carried it with him and threw it into a mailbox in the city."

"But isn't it strange?" replied Weide, "that the thieves should not have had the resources to pay the postage?"

"That may be a coincidence—I have seen such forgetfulness in this type of situation before."

"But," Weide continued, "why should the thieves have forced him to write this rather vague letter?"

"Probably because they have a specific interest in telling the public that he's alive."

"What interest would that be?"

Asbjörn Krag shrugged.

"That remains obscure and must await further developments," he said, "but it will probably clear up faster than we think."

Thomas Weide remained silent for a while, then said, "Such letters have a different character. I have seen ransom letters in my legal practice. They maintain that, if at a certain point in time, some thousands of kroner are not paid, the victim who writes the letter will suffer as a result. That's the way kidnapping works."

"That's the devil," said Krag.

"What do you mean?"

"Here's that damned little devil again, who turns all the conclusions upside down. You can see for yourself that the blackmail story would be complete, beginning with Abbot Montrose's enigmatic abduction and finishing with this letter. But then comes the contradiction: the letter contains no mention of ransom. In this case, no sooner does it begin to make sense than there is some surprising detail that undermines your theory."

"Have there been many such surprising details?" asked Weide, looking at the detective inquiringly.

"Yes, many."

"Couldn't such details become a chain? Won't they connect if you place them side by side and form their own theory?"

Krag laughed.

"I've already considered that," he said. "For the time being, however, I have only disconnected scraps; yet I collect them. So that you get an impression of the strange chaos of the whole, I want to share my thinking with you about this drama.

"The crime was apparently planned by several conspirators whose leaders worked as gardeners here, and as such, had the opportunity to familiarize themselves with the daily habits at the abbey. One, named Arnold Singer, is under arrest. I don't think I am wrong in calling him the leader of the whole affair. Now look at this room, what a wild fight took place here! Blood and ink and overturned chairs and battered furniture everywhere. Barely four hours after the crime took place, we arrested Singer, but neither his clothes nor his person revealed the slightest signs of bloodstains or even that he had been in any sort of altercation, much less the battle that apparently took place here."

"And that is devil number one," mumbled Weide.

"This circumstance, combined with his very clever statements, made his innocence look plausible. But then he himself called his own innocence into question when he made a completely meaningless escape attempt."

"So, devil number two," said Weide.

"Further," continued Krag, "why did the robbers kidnap Abbot Montrose? I assure you, the pointlessness of such an act of violence is obvious. The criminals would have needed to drag him over a tall wrought-iron fence. With the police on their heels, that seems almost impossible. Nonetheless, Abbot Montrose disappeared in the company of the thieves. Under the circumstances, I can only explain it by assuming that he went with them voluntarily, and you, who know Abbot Montrose, will probably admit the absurdity of such an assumption."

"Devil number three," murmured the lawyer.

"Suppose, however, that with the help of some inexplicable trickery the thieves really succeeded in abducting the studious and well-respected Abbot, it may have been for the sole purpose of blackmailing his friends and relatives. But then, you receive this letter in which there is no talk of ransom. Devil number four, correct?"

Weide nodded.

Asbjörn Krag meant to continue his explanation – one only truly understands a thing when one can explain it to others – when he was interrupted by the sound of hurried footsteps on the garden's gravel path.

It was Detective Keller.

He came running past the window, skidded to a halt, threw open the door and gasped, "Did you see him?"

"See who?"

"Prison Face, the man from the Gilded Peacock. He just climbed over the garden fence."

"Devil number five," said Krag, getting up.

XXII. Under the Garden Trees

"My dear Keller," said Krag, "Why are you telling me this now? Wouldn't it have been better if you had waited until you got hold of him? I am afraid that this man, 'Prison Face' as you call him, is an important personality. And he just climbed over the garden gate, you say?"

"Calm down," said Keller, laughing harshly and holding back Krag, who was on his way through the door, "it's already too late, the man has legged it into the Krydder District by now, but I've sent Officer 314 after him. Officer 314 is the best runner in the whole police squad. We must wait for a message from him. It almost seems as if Prison Face is especially interested in you, Krag. He's been following you, noticeably, at the Gilded Peacock several times already, and now he also seems to have tracked you down here at the Abbey."

Keller pointed out into the garden.

"When I came through the southern entrance to the garden," he said, "I saw him standing there among the trees and peering into the window. I crept as quietly as possible, and finally was so close that I could see his face clearly."

Keller made himself comfortable in a chair and continued, "He has a strange face. Rarely have I seen the horrors of prison—bad air, constricting walls, loneliness, and humiliation—more clearly expressed in a man's face. But his face also contained something else as he stood and stared into the window, something unspeakably vindictive, something intensely hostile and visceral; it was so conspicuous that I stiffened involuntarily. For a moment I almost panicked, it was that disturbing. But then he spotted me and ran off. With astonishing agility, he swung himself over the fence – almost like a monkey – and disappeared into the Krydder District. Fortunately, Officer 314 was close by so I waived him down through the bars and told him to follow. By the time I had made it out the gate, he would have been long gone. But now there is a chance we can still catch him. Do you have any idea why he cares so much about you, Krag?"

"No. I don't remember ever having anything to do with him. But his presence here in the garden seems strange to me. We need to make more inquiries about him."

"That's my opinion too," said Keller.

Thomas Weide, realizing his presence was superfluous, withdrew with a few polite phrases.

"Mr. Weide is Abbot Montrose's friend and legal advisor," said Krag.

"Ah, well, haven't you told him?" asked Keller. "I think you mean, *was*."

"Well, perhaps not exactly. It seem that Abbot Montrose lives."

"What? Has this been proven?"

Krag handed him the letter that Abbot Montrose had written to Weide. Keller read it carefully and remained silent for a long time.

"The more I think about it," he said finally, "the more confusing it becomes. And this letter doesn't help, my God. I received another message today, which also confuses me. I came here to talk to you about it, Krag. Do you remember the receipt for Singer's wages to which we attached so much importance?"

"Which was stolen from the police archives?"

"When I went to investigate it this morning," Keller went on, "to my astonishment, I found the receipt in the archive exactly where we had left it. The receipt has therefore not been stolen at all. Abbot Montrose made out two similar ones. Here, see for yourself."

Krag took the two notes and compared them. After thinking for a while, he said, "We've forgotten about the professor. Strantz's name starts with S., as does Singer. Both worked in Montrose's garden. It can be assumed that they were paid their weekly salary on the same day. Like all scholars, Abbot Montrose was probably a very impractical man who didn't keep ledgers but wrote his receipts on loose sheets of paper. The mad professor may have taken his receipt while Singer's stayed in the library. That seems like a natural and simple explanation."

Keller laughed loudly.

"I wish," he said, "that all the other cursed contradictions in this investigation would be equally easy to solve."

"The more complicated a thing is," said Krag, "the simpler the solution must be. Once you have found the right thread, any knot may be unraveled smoothly."

So, the two detectives sat for a long while talking to each other, each lamenting the impenetrability and obscurity of the evidence before them. But their manner of speaking revealed that their thoughts were somewhere else. As they spoke, they stared past each other distractedly, their eyes searching out into the garden. From time to time a comment was made that bore witness to the fact that they were both trying to penetrate the darkness, and that each was searching in his own way for the thread that could lead them to their destination. Sometimes they met in their train of thought. Once, one said aloud, "That he lives doesn't make things clearer."

The other replied, "No, because the letter could be several days old."

And the first one again, "That's why he might be dead."

These apparently contradictory words showed that their thoughts circled the same point. Both thought, "The letter may have been written with a specific intention and may have been forced out of the Abbot before the burglary or murder – certainly before the murder." However, no matter how many times they circled it, the matter remained wrapped in darkness.

A strong gust of wind brought a surge of fragrance through the open door. At last, Keller said, in a miserable voice, "You know, Krag, right after the incident, we stood here and stared out into the garden. I had the feeling, dear Krag, that you were looking for the secret, expecting it to suddenly emerge from the trees. Now the crowns of those trees have become fuller, just hear them rustling in the wind. Are they telling you more now? Not me. And do we know more than we did then? We have learned a great deal but it has taught us nothing. The mystery has only become more impenetrable. I hardly believe we will find a solution in this garden and under these trees."

Krag replied, "Maybe we have gotten farther than we think, but we have been unlucky. Yesterday, when we talked to Strantz, we were close to the solution. Don't you remember, as he said, 'I know where everything is.' Behind his words hides the solution of the riddle. But then death came between us."

"Death came to prevent him from saying too much," replied Keller, "and when the matter is clear, it may show an even more terrible face than we have yet assumed. Hello, what's that?"

Keller rose.

XXIII. 28 Hussars Way

A man had come staggering into the garden through the south entrance, the gate that faced the Krydder District and which Detective Keller had left open behind him.

As he stepped out of the shadows of the trees, the sunshine fell on him and the two detectives could make out the badge on his chest.

"Uniform—," said Krag.

"—314," Keller completed.

"Right," cried Krag. "Now I recognize him too. He seems to be in a hurry."

"Something important must have happened," said Keller. "Just look at how he's running. He's stirred up a whole cloud of dust."

As Number 314 rushed through the large garden, the two detectives discussed him as if they were spectators watching a race. Both were very anxious to see what news the policeman would bring, but out of old habit they hid their curiosity under a studied indifference.

When the policeman approached, Krag said "It's the same one who ran after the criminals the morning the drama started. Of course, it's not fitting to joke about such a serious matter, but doesn't it look as if he has been chasing the riddle all the time, and has now returned to the starting point with no results? Bravo 314, what news have you brought?"

Number 314 stopped in front of his two superiors and reported with halting breath, "I have to report . . . a murder . . . a murder at . . . 28 Hussars Way."

Krag and Keller both jumped, and chorused, "Arnold Singer's house!"

In fact, the new crime had taken place in the gardener's home. And the new victim was Charlie—Clary Singer's brother.

The first thought of both detectives was that Number 314 had been sent to capture the suspected person they called Prison Face, and that after some time he returned and reported a murder.

It was not surprising, that they connected one with the other, and when the three men sat in the car, driving them quickly to 28 Hussars Way, Keller asked his subordinate, "Did you get Prison Face?"

"No," said the policeman, "he escaped into the narrow streets near the Gilded Peacock."

The policeman continued, "I almost caught him, but he disappeared into the Krydder District and escaped. You know how easy it is to hide there, where the dark doorways are as close together as rat holes in an old warehouse. After hunting around there for a while, I learned from a colleague returning from a patrol duty that a person looking like Prison Face had just sneaked through Heaven Alley where the Gilded Peacock is. Knowing that this man stayed at the Peacock, I went there immediately. Just as I arrived, Prison Face was sneaking out of the gate of the Gilded Peacock. He saw me and jumped back behind the gate at the same moment. And then, I was after him."

When the policeman, who was evidently a thorough and reliable man, had come this far in his report, he tried to record something on a piece of paper despite the car's vibration. But Krag stopped him.

"I understand," he said, "you want to draw a sketch of the layout of the Peacock, but we already know it well. Through the gate you reach a courtyard full of old junk, stairs, edges, and corners."

The policeman nodded.

"Then you will understand," he said, "that it was easy for the fellow to hide from me. It took ten minutes before I realized he had escaped over a plank separating the Peacock's yard from the next yard over. If possible, this yard is even more angular and dirtier than the first one. And from there a narrow passage leads to the remnants of an old garden, and the garden leads to a new jumble of backyards and building sites, which adjoin the small workers' dwellings on Hussars Way. In this way one can, if one follows all these angles and passages, pass through the whole stinking mass of houses, which separate Heaven Alley from Hussars Way—at least, if one possesses enough local knowledge. And that my fellow seemed to have, as I regret to admit."

"It seems to be a thoroughfare for criminals," Keller remarked bitterly, remembering his own defeat, "the same way two murderers had escaped yesterday."

The policeman continued, "When I finally stood in the backyard at 28 Hussars Way, all I could say was that Prison Face had long since escaped. My search through the hustle and bustle of various backyards had taken at least fifteen minutes."

Krag, who wanted to determine the time, asked, "Are you sure Prison Face was fifteen minutes ahead?"

"At least," replied the policeman, thinking. "Maybe it was twenty minutes. And after I found out, I gave up the chase. But then something occurred, which set me on the trail of the new crime. As I said earlier, I was in the backyard at 28 Hussars Way. While I was still standing, wondering if I should go back to the Gilded Peacock to at least learn something about Prison Face, something very surprising happened. A frantic woman suddenly appeared in one of the open windows of the house, stretching out her arms and crying desperately for help. She was a young, beautiful woman who was on the verge of falling out the window, showing all the signs of utter horror. I came nearer and saw the cause of her confusion: on the sofa in the room lay the body of a murdered man."

"And the woman was Clary Singer?" Krag asked.

"Yes," answered the policeman, "and the murdered man was her brother. But now, Detectives, we are at our destination. This is 28 Hussars Way."

The police car was immediately surrounded by a staring, curious, and frightened crowd. The news had already spread through the neighborhood. Many people had gathered. Outside the small garden fence stood an empty doctor's car. The gate was being guarded by a brusque police officer in a tight-fitting uniform. There were people of all ages, the sort of crowd that always gathers when something serious has happened—a conflagration, a crime, or an accident of some sort. There stood the barefoot urchin with his spin top, serious, and yet vacant, with his mouth hanging open, surrounded by little children who barely dared to whisper to each other; red-cheeked women, their fat, bare arms folded across their chests; workers from the new building nearby, some with their tools in hand, others without hats, proof of the haste with which they had left their work. One saw the types of passersby, as one usually encounters in crowds on the street: the fine gray-bearded gentleman with the top hat, who had been out for a walk; the telegraph messenger, who has gotten off his bike; the distraught old lady, who has already taken out her handkerchief; the man in the wheelchair relentlessly left to his fate—all mingling without distinction into a whispering, frightened, questioning crowd. Far, far down the road, you can see a man on wings of dust, a messenger to remote parts of the city, where the news has yet to arrive.

The air was foggy, and a cold wind prophesying rain tore at the trees of the little garden. The open windows of number 28 appeared unnaturally black and yawning, with that threatening expression that windows have in a house where an accident has happened, or a fire has just been extinguished. Inside, the curtains fluttered like dark shadows.

XXIV. Flowers and Dirty Fingers

For the second time Asbjörn Krag appeared in Arnold Singer's small home.

With the awareness of the tiniest details that is characteristic of detectives, he immediately grasped how clean and tidy everything was. It looked as if the anxiety and excitement of the last few days had not in the least affected the young woman's sense of order. Even fresh flowers stood on the shelves . . .

Flowers! Krag froze on the threshold, staring. They were unusually numerous and unusually beautiful. It was not until the doctor approached Krag that the detective was able to tear himself away from his admiration, an admiration that Keller found so inappropriate that he looked at his friend reproachfully.

The doctor said, "There is nothing left to do here. He was shot through the temple which was instantly fatal. I'll submit my detailed report later."

"Who sent for you?" Krag asked.

The doctor pointed to the next room.

"That one, in there," he said, "a big, fat man, his father, I gather."

As Krag entered the next room, Keller began to examine the dead man.

Krag stopped in the door and scanned the room.

It was a bit smaller than the first, apparently a kind of parlor in a very modest style. The room had two windows, one to the street and one to the yard. In the window to the yard, Number 314 had seen Clary Singer hysterically shouting for help. Both windows were open, and the damp wind swept through the room, making the mood inside even more uncomfortable. The light was failing, the rain not far away. The doctor had gone, and except for Krag and Keller, only two people were in the room. One was the proprietor of the Gilded Peacock, the gigantic restaurateur, Whist, aka The Raincloud, who blocked the window with his immense body, and who, when he saw Asbjörn Krag, literally swelled with rage and screamed, "You! You—you!"

With these words he expressed as clearly as he could his disgust and regret over what had happened. The vocabulary of this colossus seemed unusually limited. Since he was unable to create a large enough outflow of words to express his feelings, he seemed ready to burst.

Krag came up to him and let his fingers disappear into a damp crease near the Raincloud's arm that may have been a hand.

"We are here to find out what happened and to avenge the crime," he said, "so you needn't be angry with us."

"No, no," grumbled the Raincloud, "but ever since I saw your face in the Peacock, it has been one misfortune after another."

"That's hardly fair," replied Krag, "much had happened before I showed myself there."

Krag knew that the Raincloud would only half understand this remark, but he nonetheless looked him in the eye. The Raincloud's eyes shone grimly, as always, in that huge and unnatural head, but at the same time they expressed a certain helplessness.

Krag then turned to the second person in the room.

Clary Singer stood leaning exhausted against the window frame, while trying to hold back the fluttering curtain with her trembling hands.

Krag gently took her by the wrist and led her carefully into the next room, where Number 314 waited. She let herself be led willingly, as if she had a certain confidence in him.

"Can you explain what happened?" asked the detective.

She only shook her head.

"No," she answered helplessly. "I had gone out to fetch milk for my daughter who was sleeping in the bedroom. Charlie was lying on the sofa reading. He had just come back from the police department; he must check in every day. I came back with the milk, opened the door to the bedroom and the child was still asleep. She is still sleeping now. Do you want to see her?"

"No," answered Krag, "let her sleep. What happened next?"

"Then I sat at the window, where I've been sitting since you took Arnold. I sit at the window and look out into the street, because I still expect him to come back at any moment. I know Arnold has nothing to do with any of this business. I know, because I know him. If the police knew him better, they would understand it too; if you knew him, then . . . "

"This isn't about Arnold," Krag interrupted, "but about your murdered brother. How did you discover the murder? Did you hear something?"

"No," she replied, "on the contrary, I heard nothing, I didn't even hear that he was turning the pages of his book, everything was deathly quiet. It must have happened while I was gone. The silence made me uneasy. It was quiet . . . too quiet. You don't know how appalling it is to wait hour after hour, and to be unable to sleep at night, no, you don't know how terrible it is when everything around you is silent . . . deathly quiet. As I sat there, I became uneasy because I didn't hear him turn the pages, and finally I called to him, 'Charlie, are you asleep?' But he didn't answer. Then I thought, 'He must be sleeping.' And again, I sat for a long while, listening for his breathing. But I didn't hear anything. The door was open, and I thought maybe he had gone out. I went to the door and peeked in, and suddenly I thought I was having a terrible dream, for he lay on the ground with his feet on the sofa, and blood was spilling from his forehead to the carpet. After that, I remember nothing until I stood by the window and screamed until the policeman came up to me . . ."

She spoke with the sort of hysterical voice that women fall into during a nervous fit. Her eyes were wide and distraught.

Krag ordered her to go in to her child's room and stay there until further notice. He also had the door guarded by Number 314 to prevent her from doing anything rash.

Meanwhile, in the small parlor, Keller had made a careful examination of the dead man.

"Look here," he said as Krag came in, "a violent but short fight has taken place, the murdered man's clothes are torn open at his chest, and his shirt is tattered. The dead man's face reflects an intense fright. That isn't the most important thing, though; the most important thing is that the killer has left distinct prints on his shirt. Finally, some evidence. What do you think . . ."

Keller stopped, transfixed.

"You are sniffing the air like a dog," he said. "Why?"

"The most important thing," Asbjörn Krag answered absently, "perhaps the most important thing is this strange fragrance. Don't you remember it from the Crazy Professor's room? It's the same scent and the same flowers."

XXV. The Child and the Murder

Keller hesitated. He had to agree with Krag. There were an unusual number of beautiful and fragrant flowers in the small home. When Krag had been here the previous time, he had seen the flowers as well, but he had thought that the quiet, sympathetic young woman had a fondness for beautiful flowers and he left the idea there. But now the scent of the flowers evoked with intense clarity the memory of the sour, almost cemetery-like scent of flowers in Strantz's room. Even now, the scent of flowers enveloped the murdered man. Perhaps this was the reason that the vivid color of the flowers suddenly seemed so eerie, and with such forcefulness evoked the idea of the nearness of death.

"The same flowers," murmured Krag. "Look, there are those red Japanese roses on the mantel, just like the flowers in Strantz's apartment."

"I admit that there is a strange coincidence between these flowers and this murdered man," said Keller, "but the flowers themselves don't seem to me to be inexplicable. They are all from the abbey's greenhouse."

"No doubt."

"It's not just the Crazy Professor who stole flowers, Singer has been stealing them as well."

Krag didn't answer. For a long time, he couldn't tear his eyes away from the flowers, seemingly lost in reverie. Engrossed in their bright colors and smelling the fragrance that ran through his head like the breath of tombs and cemetery chapels, he felt that there was something, some thread, that would explain everything that now seemed so mysterious.

Meanwhile, Keller, ever practical, was absorbed in inspecting the dead man and the fingerprints that seemed to interest him far more than the flowers that adorned the apartment.

From the dirty fingerprints the criminal had left on the windowsill, it was easy for Keller to see that the murderer had come into the room that way. Probably Charlie had tried to disarm him and a fierce, short fight had broken out during which Charlie had been killed by a shot to the head from close range. The killer had then quietly left the room through the door.

Keller explained all this to Krag with great zeal. To identify the killer, he tore off a piece of Charlie's shirt covered with fingerprints and carefully placed it in his pocketbook.

The innkeeper listened with increasing agitation and interest to the detectives' conversation, while they stood muttering, searching the dead man, and examining with a magnifying glass the spots on the white-polished surface of the windowsill. He heard them say, "He must have come from there."

"He saw Charlie through the open window."

"The shot must have been fired while the policeman was looking for him near the Peacock."

Then the Raincloud growled angrily, "Is the Peacock guilty of this murder too, gentlemen?"

Krag answered him, "You seem to be more worried about your hotel than about your son?"

"He's dead," the Raincloud answered with a logic none of the others understood. And he added, "Besides, he's only just gotten out of jail. He never wanted to work properly. Maybe death will protect him from ending up there again."

"Do you know if he had any enemies?"

"I know neither his enemies nor his friends."

"Who sent for you?"

"I suppose it was one of the officers. When I got here, I phoned the doctor."

Krag asked him to take his daughter and granddaughter home with him.

"Glad to," grumbled the Raincloud bitterly and wistfully, "and she should stay there. I should never have given her away. All misfortune stems from when she left me to go with that painter."

"Painter?" asked Krag. "Do you mean the gardener, Singer?"

"You can call him a gardener as well. He never had a steady job. When he came to me, he was a painter. It is he who has painted all the peacocks in my hotel. He's gone now. The police have already got him, and they cannot get him anymore. I'm going now and taking my daughter with me, at least they won't get her nor me either, even if they send ten thousand devils after us to bring us to misery."

It had been a long time since the thunderstorm had been so powerfully discharged, and he was breathing laboriously after the effort.

Krag held him back by the sleeve.

"Just a minute," he said. "Did Arnold Singer really paint the peacocks?"

"Yes."

"Well done," he said, "a great painting talent, unusual and a little degenerate, yet significant."

Krag commented on flowers and art, as if he were giving his opinion at an exhibition. It sounded strange in this terribly disturbed place, where police helmets flashed, a frightened crowd waited in the rainy weather outside the fluttering curtains, a bloody corpse lay in the room, and the desperate weeping of a woman could be heard. Krag still stood admiring the flowers as Clary, with the child in her arms and accompanied by the colossus, left the apartment. Just as she was about to cross the threshold, the child awoke and wrapped her round arms around her mother's neck. Her eyes, which were shiny with health and sleep, were caught by the flashing brass of the helmets. In her childlike expression, showing innocence and play, the contrast between the pious beginning of life and its serious and degenerate development almost reached the sublime. When the child was gone, the misery in this ruined home seemed doubly meaningless.

But police officers see so much that it doesn't touch them anymore. That's why it wasn't difficult for Keller to resume his police-like dialogue.

"The murder took place in the fifteen minutes during which Clary Singer had gone to fetch milk. It was in this quarter of an hour that Officer 314 was chasing Prison Face through the neighborhood towards this very spot. Prison Face must have been here. He probably saw the killer, or he was the killer himself."

"Agreed," said Krag.

"And since we have the fingerprints," Keller continued, "it will be easy for us to determine to what extent the latter assumption is correct."

Before an hour had passed, they were clear about the following:

The fingerprints on the murdered man's shirt were those of a man recently released from jail for a robbery attempt.

The name of the man was Georges.

When they looked up photographs in the criminal records, it turned out that Georges's face was identical to that of Prison Face.

So, Charlie had been murdered by the man Number 314 had been chasing. This result was half what the detectives expected.

What they didn't expect, however, was the additional information provided by the criminal records, which included:

Georges, born 1879, former helmsman on the *Eddystone* . . .

"Helmsman, I would have sworn he was a deck hand," said Keller, "the way he could climb."

"*Eddystone*," said Asbjörn Krag thoughtfully. "Now we have returned to the storyteller and the bright Spanish colors. For Hans Christian Andersen has disappeared from the *Eddystone*, not the author of *The Ugly Duckling*, but his namesake Hans Christian Andersen, owner of the scarf from Bilbao."

XXVI. The Fingers

In a visit to the prison, they also learned that Georges had been released about one month ago after serving his sentence. His behavior had not been exemplary during his prison term; he had been disciplined several times, the last time because of an escape attempt. The prison priest provided testimony that Georges was an unusually reserved, defiant, and contentious person. His incarceration had had no good influence on him whatsoever, the priest wrote, adding, "Perhaps the loss of freedom to this man, who had enjoyed complete freedom on all the seas of the world from his earliest youth, became morally oppressive—"

Now it was time to capture Georges, and the detectives were hoping that they would find him soon. The police had spread the word everywhere, and a man with such a pronounced appearance could not keep himself hidden for long.

A curious circumstance in the most recent murder was that the detectives could not be certain about whether it was an intentional murder or self-defense.

What else had Georges in mind when he spied on Krag and Thomas Weide in Abbot Montrose's garden?

Was there any connection between Georges, the tragedy of Montrose, and the murder of the poor drunken Strantz? What supported the assumption that he was involved in this affair?

One of Strantz's killers belonged to the crew of the *Eddystone*. Prison Face used to be a helmsman aboard this ship.

Prison Face had been seen in the corridor of the Gilded Peacock just before Strantz's murder.

All these details could not possibly be accidental.

To top things off, he also fled from Number 314. Fleeing from the police might almost be a habit with someone like Prison Face but it did, nonetheless, suggest a guilty conscience.

Now, however, came the contradictions (so the detectives assumed). Did Georges kill Charlie because he was being chased by the police and because Charlie was preventing his escape through Hussars Way?

Or had Georges accidentally discovered Charlie and had a definite, pre-existing reason to shoot him down?

The detectives were inclined to think the latter, although Georges had apparently made no attempt to force an entry through the front door (the gate was locked but not bolted); he had gone straight to the open window. Charlie, lying on the sofa and reading, could easily be seen from the yard.

Here Asbjörn Krag, added the following general considerations, "There is every indication that Georges had come to Arnold Singer's yard through a series of coincidences. Because he was being chased by the policeman, he had been sneaking from street to street and finally from backyard to backyard. Of course, he knows the secret paths through the old quarter that separates Heaven Alley from Hussars Way. He knows he can pass through the gate of Arnold Singer's house to Hussars Way. But when he comes into the yard, he sees Charlie through the open window lying in on the sofa. Forgetting his own dangerous situation, forgetting that he could escape through the gate, he is seized by a sudden, all-consuming idea that he wants to murder the man lying there. And he carries out his purpose, although he knows that a policeman is on his heels. That he escapes anyway, is down to luck, not skill. Why did he commit this murder?"

Keller, who was absorbed in the prison priest's report and the fingerprints protocol, had only half listened to Krag.

Now he looked up.

"I've always imagined," he said, "that a maniacal murderer would behave in exactly that way."

"A madman?" murmured Krag. "That would require any assumption that Georges is involved in the tragedy of Montrose be set aside. Besides, it is an old superstition that madmen with mania for murder act in such a way. If it was Georges intention or, if you prefer, his instinct to kill, then it would have been more likely that he would have faced the policeman who was pursuing him with his revolver in his hand. No, I am sure that Georges has been sane the whole time. Initially it was only his intention to escape the policeman; but then, when he reached the backyard of Arnold Singer's house, he saw Charlie through the open window—and driven by a momentary inspiration, he acted."

"What inspiration?" asked Keller.

"The inspiration that seizes a man when he sees he is finally at his destination."

"Do you think Charlie was the target?"

"Charlie's death was the target."

"Then why didn't he kill him earlier?"

"Because he had not found him earlier."

"Do you think he followed us because he thought he'd find Charlie in our company?"

Krag didn't answer. He just shrugged his shoulders—a gesture that can mean both that you know nothing and that you know a lot.

"Why did Charlie have to die?"

The same meaningful or meaningless gesture.

"It is strange," continued Keller, "while we have been addressing the original crime, with Abbot Montrose's enigmatic disappearance, one unexpected event after another has overtaken us. But as soon as the events have arrived, it turns out that they are all connected with each other, that they intertwine, like the leaves in a wreath. But what does it mean that we haven't been able to see any of this coming, and that murder after murder has unexpectedly fallen upon us? That means nothing else, dear Krag, than that we are still completely in the dark. And in this damned hopeless situation, in despair, we resort to the most meaningless explanations. Do you know what I thought at the moment when I saw the traces of the murderer's fingers on Charlie's shirt?"

"You thought for a moment," answered Krag, "that they were the traces of Abbot Montrose's fingers."

"Yes," confessed Keller, looking up.

Krag began to grin."You laugh," said Keller softly.

Krag became serious again. He jumped as if awakened from deep musing.

XXVII. The Hunt

This conversation took place in Keller's private office in the detective department. For the last few minutes, bells had been ringing incessantly in the adjoining rooms.

Krag went and stood by the door.

"The police are starting to take phone calls, it seems," he said, consulting his watch. "We can expect the first news reports now."

He nodded and started to leave but stopped. "No, I didn't laugh," he said.

"It seemed to me that you did," replied Keller, "but it was also a wild idea of mine."

"You are right," said Krag. "In a situation like this one falls for the strangest ideas, and it was not my intention to treat you with scorn. I must confess, I didn't even know what you said, I only heard the sound of your words. And if I twisted my mouth a little, it only meant that I was laughing in meditation, as if listening to distant music."

Keller got up forcefully and struck the paper-covered table with the flat of his hand.

"No, now you are being too poetic," he cried, half joking, half angry. "All you talk about are roses and fairy tales, and now music. What do you mean by this last remark?"

"Oh, nothing special," replied Krag good-naturedly. "I just wanted to say figuratively that I have an idea . . . that I feel like I am listening to distant music that I can't quite make out or smelling the scent of flowers that I cannot see. I am not a poet, but I wish that I could express my feelings in the indefinite and indefinable form of a poet, when I suspect that my mind is in the process of capturing the right, the light, the solution. A poet who has long

135

struggled with the completion of a work and suddenly feels a sense of release, not clearly and palpably, but with a sense of anticipation and growth, feels what I feel now. He knows he has the whole poem in his head, somewhere, and all that remains is to release it out into the world. Now I just need to collect everything, Keller, and I have the solution, the light. It's all in my head, somewhere. It's a very strange affair."

Keller didn't remember ever having seen his friend so excited – or indeed, so poetical, despite his denials – and he studied him with a concern approaching alarm.

***

Krag walked down the long corridor that connected the detectives' hall to the iron staircase leading to the jail cells.

In the corridor, he met a plainclothes policeman whose trousers were held together with bicycle clips at the ankle. He led the policeman into a large room, where several other detectives sat and waited at a large table covered by a green cloth. It was the meeting room of the violent crime unit, full of telephones and manuals, but otherwise poorly furnished; except for the big table, there were just a few uncomfortable chairs and a huge closet.

While the detective who had entered in front of him went to the telephone, Asbjörn Krag began a conversation with the other detectives. One of them left after receiving a short message from Krag; others arrived including a clerk in uniform who came in with papers, which he placed on the green table, whereupon he disappeared again. Meanwhile, the phones rang with their sharp crackling metallic sounds. A man in a prison guard uniform came in with a letter he handed to Krag, which he kept unopened after glancing at it. A heavy policeman, sighing because of the warmth in the room and unbuttoning his uniform, put a large red-bordered poster on the table. Krag looked at it and nodded in approval. It was a "Wanted" poster depicting Prison Face—a sign that was meant to be posted on every streetlight in the city. In the meeting room, only short and quiet words were exchanged. Nobody said anything superfluous. Every now and then you heard the "Hello! Hello!" of the officials on the telephone. That's what the meeting room looked like on a day when murder was being investigated, or when something unusual was going on. There was an intense bustle, but no confusion. An incessant coming and going of men whose appearance in no way coincides with the common notion one has of detectives. Strong men of military caliber, clear-eyed and alert, returning by bike and departing again.

The only one who distanced himself from these men was Asbjörn Krag, who took his favorite position at the window, his back to the light, reading the letter he had just received. His eyes, behind pince-nez, were more expressive, his features more refined; with his bald head he looked more like a judge or an accountant, than a detective.

Such was the life in this uncomfortable, spare, yellow room with the bare windows, a life that expressed concentrated, purposeful activity, intense pursuit. Outside in the gray stone desert of the city, however, one could sense a wildness; somewhere, the murderer hid in the crowd and in the dark shadows, quivering with anticipation of death, eyes filled with a savage determination.

If an unauthorized person had come to the headquarters of the violent crime unit during these hours and listened for a while to the orders and fragments of the conversation, he would very soon have concluded that they were working here according to a specific plan.

Meanwhile Krag answered a telephone call and one could hear him saying, "Take the inns on B Street, and then all the sailors' pubs on the wharf."

Or, "You have been to the sailor's lodging house? Good. There is also a home for Christian sailors at Victoria Wharf, go there too."

Or, "Send Johnson to the steamships."

Or, "Arrange that no sailing ships leave."

Then the man on the telephone shouted through the room, "Pat found a trail on the coal quay but lost it again."

Krag, who was talking to the police chief, just nodded. The chief had come to the criminal unit for a moment to see for himself how things were progressing. He was nervous. The reputation of the entire police department was at stake. He already felt the unrestrained excitement of the newspaper editors. He didn't take part in the investigation himself, but as the chief, he was responsible. In an hour he was due to have lunch with the minister and he wanted – here Krag recognized his vanity and smiled – to share the news of the arrest at lunch, as any mighty chief of police loves to communicate such news, unaffectedly casual, with a frosty, gray policeman's gaze, "Dear Mrs. X. We caught the killer at 6:34 a.m."

And Krag said, "He can't escape us, sir, we are on his trail, I think I can almost hear his fleeing steps. He (Krag gestured with his head toward the officer with the bicycle clips) said that after the murder, Georges didn't return to the small room he lives in. He didn't dare, because he knows we're after him. Incidentally, I fully expect him to confess when he is eventually captured."

"Really," said the chief of police astonished. "Why do you think so?"

"Because of his motive."

Krag laid his hand on the letter he had just received.

"I have the motive here," he said. "The poor man may have believed he could escape. He is a longtime sailor and knows that sailors are in short supply at this time and many a distressed captain will turn to secret methods to sign up a man. Maybe he also knows some unscrupulous person who would be willing to help him. But our people are everywhere. Every ship has been instructed, every hiring office, sailor's home, every pub. Maybe he's hesitating because he's scared, but he'll be with us soon."

"I will await more news in my office," said the chief. "Please call me immediately."

And the intense activity in the police investigation room continued. People came and went. The reports followed each other.

Finally, the moment came that many people recognize from other circumstances in their lives. The moment when one notices—from a violent jolt of the expressions of life around him, the waning activity, and the hasty breathing—that a decision has been made.

Suddenly a bell rang with unusual brightness, and all the voices mingled in a many-voiced murmur as a dusty and sweaty cyclist came rushing into the room; the door was thrown open, and remained wide open, so that many steps could be heard in the corridor. All eyes turned towards the newcomer who stood in the midst of a spreading pool of silence.

"We got him."

XXVIII. The Lashes

He sat in a cell in Police Department B, down by the harbor. He had timidly come to the hiring office of the Sailor's Mission, his cap in his hand, and asked in a hoarse voice if an experienced sailor might be hired. He was arrested immediately by a detective who was already there and waiting. He just said, "Fine." and he had not spoken again since. He had been relieved of a revolver with four bullets inside. Now he was sitting on the bench behind the bars of his cell, hunched over, arms on his knees. From time to time he looked up at the policeman and stretched out his body, a movement with which he silently expressed a sort of defiant self-abandonment. The policemen treated him graciously, as the police always treat prey when it has been captured and is in their power. He was given coffee and bread, which he gobbled desperately. Tobacco was offered to him, which he didn't accept.

When one of his guards asked him, "Why did you shoot the poor fellow?" he answered, "Because he deserved it." Then he stubbornly stretched and said nothing more.

Soon after Krag came in and sat beside him on the bench outside the bars of the holding cell. He kept his raincoat on but had his felt hat in his hand. He had come alone in a car from the police station.

"You did clean work," Krag told him.

Georges raised himself up and moved slightly to the side of the bench to avoid being so close to the detective.

"Oh, yes, it was well done," he said, laughing. A strange laugh in that grayish, immobile face.

139

The faint sound of rolling cars and the tram bell came half-stifled through the thick walls. The thought blazed through Krag's head like a flash of lightning: the city outside, thousands of people, were now busy talking about this sensational murder. The story rebounded through a mile-long bustle of streets. It echoed, "The killer, the killer. . . Do you have him? Where is he?" Like a cataclysm that threatens death, or a sinister symbol that everyone can see. . . the entire population is obsessed by a shared, frenzied desire for some news of this one human being. "Where is he? Through which of our countless busy streets do his menacing steps echo?"

And now he's sitting here in this narrow, gloomy room, lit by a blue gas flame that hangs from a freshly whitewashed ceiling, and wearing a smile on his dirty, unbelievably tired face with its brown, tobacco-stained teeth. Krag said to him, "If things had been different, I would have liked to see you escape to sea, aboard a sailing ship, for example. Imagine being on a rocking deck right now as the beacons disappear behind you."

"It's better this way," said Georges, swinging his cap. "How long will it be?"

"What?"

"Until I'm hanged?"

"Maybe you won't be hanged at all. It depends."

"No, that's impossible," replied Georges, "impossible. I'll hang."

He looked around the room like someone just waking up and his eyes came to rest on the revolver on the table.

Asbjörn Krag made a sign and the police officer put the revolver in his pocket.

"It's not supposed to tempt you again," the detective said kindly to Georges.

Prison Face bowed his head and let out a low hum that seemed to come from the bottom of his chest.

Krag now requested he be left alone with the prisoner, and the two police officers stumped out, although they would have liked to attend the interrogation. One took a piece of paper and the other a record book. Neither of these had any connection to the prisoner or the investigation, but this is the way people who are forced to leave a room tend to behave.

Prison Face understood that the interrogation was about to commence and became restless. He moved further away from Krag. They sat and talked like two strangers who happened to be sitting side by side in the waiting room of a train station. This comparison came to Asbjörn Krag's mind when he saw the shiny, yellow fresh-washed bench. When the conversation was over, they would part, and each would board their own train. Krag would return to life and to all that it offered, but the other man had only the irrevocable final journey into nothingness. They were the same age, but one was free and the other was marked. One triumphed, the other sat trembling, waiting for death, and struggling with a strange harsh cough that resembled a suppressed cry.

Krag asked, "Were you in the Montrose Abbey garden today?"

"Yes."

"Why?"

"Because I was looking for him, the scoundrel. I knew that he was involved in the matter with the priest. And then I thought, 'Sooner or later he will probably show up in the company of the detectives. And then it's my turn.'"

"Don't you regret your act?"

"No."

"Would you do it again?"

"Yes."

"What had you done before you committed the murder? Why did you run away from the police officer?"

"I was afraid they would arrest me again. With a suspicious person who looks like me, they don't tend to be fussy."

"So, it was just a coincidence that you spotted Charlie Whist behind the window?"

"Yes."

"With what do you want to defend yourself against the charges?"

"With nothing. I want to make my case as poor as possible."

"A murder of revenge is a deliberate act, so you can't make it much better. You are welcome to admit the truth."

The killer straightened up again and leaned back, as if breathing was hard for him; when he exhaled, the air rattled softly in his chest. How clearly did that arduous breathing express his torment, his hopelessness, and at the same time his fierce self-assertion!

Suddenly he tore his jacket and his shirt off his shoulders. Over his bare skin ran the broad traces of a lash. Krag gazed at Prison Face with compassion, as if seeing him for the first time. But the prisoner's eyes held a desperate question, a mute indictment of an unprecedented insult that only death could avenge.

"I was put in prison," said the man, "because I attacked a common rascal."

"But why didn't you endure the prison sentence with patience, without attempting escape?"

"Who doesn't seize a favorable opportunity if one is offered? I had such an opportunity. Our flight would have been successful if we had not been betrayed by that wretched worm Charlie."

"I know all that," interrupted Krag, eager to calm the man. "The prison director wrote to me. Charlie, who was in a cell with you, betrayed you. You had to undergo disciplinary punishment. You were whipped, which was tough, but fair. Remember, there are two thousand criminals in jail, murderers among them, who shy away from nothing."

Georges had not listened to him at all. He needed to vent his anger about the humiliation, the mortal abuse he had suffered.

"Why did that fat, bow-legged villain betray us? To get a better bed and cigarettes and white bread to go with his coffee? Oh, how happy I was when I grabbed him. I could see from the shock in his eyes that he understood everything. Why should I spare him? I still often dream of the room with the thick walls and the doctor, who would examine me to determine how many strokes of the whip I could stand, me, an honest sailor, no . . . "

He shook his head and pursed his lips.

"No, it's a good thing," he said, "I have no regrets."

Krag now let the other policemen come in again and told them to take the prisoner to a cell. When the detective was about to leave the room, he said as if by chance to the prisoner, "You were a helmsman aboard the *Eddystone*. Do you know a sailor named Hans Christian Andersen?"

"Yes. He is not a good man, he's ashore now, I saw him the other day in the Peacock, where he has a girl, the redhead, Dora."

"Did you talk to him?"

"No."

"For the time being I have nothing more to ask you," said Krag gently, "I wish you the peace and quiet that you require."

Krag sent the car away and walked back to the police station. He wanted to get something off his heart that distracted him deeply. When he wandered through the city with his collar up, his hands in his pockets, in the rainy, dark evening, he could not free himself from the sad reflections on the ruthless coincidences of life that invaded his thoughts. He saw Clary's uncomprehending and pained eyes in front of him and thought he heard her desperate sobbing. He saw the eyes of the murderer, Georges, with their hopelessly questioning look, and he thought he heard the strange rattling sounds from Georges's sunken chest.

At the same time, His Excellence, the chief of police, would be so happy to be able to tell his partner at the minister's dinner party, "Madam! We caught the murderer at seven o'clock."

These words, spoken among that polite company, would be a sensation; everyone would fall silent and look with unconcealed admiration at the refined gentleman with the steel gray gaze.

But it was never that easy.

XXIX. The Viscount

A man of about thirty, short in stature, thin, dark, and elegant, almost dressed as a dandy, entered the detective office.

It was eight o'clock in the evening.

"I have been looking for you since yesterday evening, my dear Viscount," said Asbjörn Krag. "Where the hell have you been?"

The viscount lowered himself onto the hard police couch, looking as if he was sitting down on a Turkish divan, and suppressed a yawn with all his energy.

"I am very tired," he said.

Krag stood in front of him and looked down at him with a humorous glint in his eye.

"I'm afraid you take your job too seriously," he said. "If you continue this way, you will not be able to do it much longer. You left your house at six o'clock yesterday afternoon, and I suppose you're coming straight from the Dance Palace."

"On the contrary, dear friend," said the viscount, "I have come straight from home. I went to bed this afternoon at five o'clock, so you can figure that I slept for two and a half hours. I'm really tired, but I'll wake up very soon, especially," he added with interest, "if I have anything to do."

Here it is necessary to make some remarks about the man whom Krag called Viscount.

Maybe he was a viscount, maybe not. At the police station, however, he was known only by this name. He distinguished himself by his noble bearing, but even more by his carelessness. The invoices, which he submitted to accounting, brought the old cashier to near tears. But as he was a merry and amiable man, all liked him and treated him half indulgently, half humorously—as one treats a bright and bold child. At the same time, they also respected him, because he was not only reckless, but also courageous, and clever. Several times he had done great service for the police. He was used in such cases where stolid police work would not serve, but where, instead, a more lithe, elegant nature was needed. In the clubs, where no one suspected that he was working for the police, he acted as a natural guest, drifting cheerfully along in the current of Bohemian life, where he was considered a sculptor, and in the demimonde where he was the darling of all because of his good mood and his dapper appearance. He had many names. He was called the Viscount by the police, in the art circles he was called Pol—this name followed him into the dance halls and cabarets, and in the clubs, he went by the name de Blondel. It sounds paradoxical but it was nonetheless true that he was no mystery to those who only knew him briefly. In the clubs, a young nobleman. In Bohemian circles, a prospective artist with money in his pocket. In the dance halls, a young bon vivant. But for those who knew him better, he was a mystery. As an undercover police officer, he earned a good living and received ample reward money, yet they knew his private life devoured much larger sums than his legitimate work brought him.

Keller once said to him, "Viscount, why are you making such trouble for yourself? You could live without a care on your own fortune."

To which the viscount replied, "You have no idea how terribly boring it is to merely have fun."

With some justification it could therefore be assumed that the viscount had sought employment with the police to kill a few hours. His challenge in life seemed to be coping with boredom. He had already gone through the whole list of pleasures and pastimes until he had come to the conclusion that pleasure itself was a source of ennui. And so, he looked for other sensations. The term "work" had been a

146

sensation to him for some time, until he had found the utmost potency of it in the unpredictable, nerve-wracking needs of the police.

Now Krag negotiated with this man. The viscount sat slumped in his spring overcoat and bobbed his patent-leather boot up and down as he listened to Krag. His eyes were half closed, his hair clung to his forehead. At that moment, when he seemed to be half asleep, one could see that, despite his youth, he had been devastated by his boredom.

"If I understand you correctly," he said, "I should go to Dora at the Peacock. Hah, I know her, she drinks like a sponge and screams so terribly."

"You must find a way."

"I will. By the way, have you noticed that all the criminal women are called Dora? Why aren't they called Cecilia? I dare say that parents who name their daughters Dora take on a terrible responsibility. If I ever have a daughter, I'll name her Cecilia. By doing so, I will have done everything within my powers to save her from a life of crime.

"So tonight, I will attend to Dora. God, how she will be delighted! But first, I'll go to the Grand Hotel and enjoy soup, champagne, an old cognac for coffee, a whiskey or two to build up my courage and strength. Then I'll hurry off to Dora!"

"Don't think about the money."

Pol tiredly raised his eyes.

"I probably will not have time for that. Dora will give me enough to think about. By the way, Dora thinks a lot about money."

"But don't forget that her friend, our teller of fairy tales, is a dangerous criminal whom we must get hold of—through Dora."

Pol was apparently already engrossed in his calculations. Half to himself, he said, "I assume Hans Christian Andersen will not be in the bar. The girls' real friends don't take part in the evening amusements.

He will float in the background. Every now and then one might hear his voice in the house, like a threatening murmur behind the wall. I will act as if I were intoxicated, very intoxicated, although it is a bit exhausting. Then home with Dora, we will take champagne with us. . . in a closed automobile, no, better open . . . bravo! Then I will fall asleep on the sofa. Dora will touch me tentatively. I will jump up and make a terrible noise. There will be a threatening, coarse male voice behind the wall. I won't surrender but will pour champagne over Dora's head. Dora will scream. The door will be torn open and the writer of fairy tales will storm in. I will play the role of a senseless drunk, be thrown down the stairs, and out into the street, where I will beg a few police officers to assist Dora—if, that is, they can be spared from the pile that arrest me. But I will point fiercely to a wrong house number, while Dora and her fairy-tale writer stand behind the curtain and laugh. Half an hour later, I will be taken to the police station, where I will suddenly become sober and say to you, 'Dear Krag, the address is 32 Pelican Street'. . . theoretically."

Krag patted his shoulder encouragingly.

"That's right," he said, "by all means, give full flight to your artistic talents."

"But," muttered Pol, lowering his head thoughtfully, "it might be that Dora will fall in love with me, that would not be . . . bravo."

Suddenly he got up.

"Anyway, I'm going to plunge headlong into the affair. Just tell me one thing. Will you be around?"

"Maybe," Krag answered.

"Then I will say goodbye."

But as Pol reached for the door, Keller came rushing into the room and made the unexpected announcement that the prisoner, Arnold Singer, had expressed the wish to make a confession.

XXX. Before the Decision

Keller looked triumphant as he made this announcement, and behind him stood a jailer with a rattling bunch of keys. The jailer nodded.

"Yes, that's right," he said. "I send the regards of the prisoner in cell 42 and he would like to make a confession. During the last few days he has been quiet and withdrawn, apparently he regrets this and wants to relieve his conscience."

"Why doesn't he want to go before the examining magistrate?" Krag asked.

"Because he doesn't want to make his confession in front of the judge, but in his cell."

"And in front of the prelate?"

"He doesn't want to talk to a priest."

"But why Keller?" Krag asked. This announcement had apparently come as a surprise.

"Of course, because he has confidence in me," interposed Keller, not without a certain pride.

The jailer nodded, "The prisoner did say he expressly wished to confide in Mr. Keller."

"Does he know him?"

"No, he just said he wanted to talk to the detective in the yellow khaki suit."

Krag looked at Keller, who was wearing a yellow-brown khaki suit of a type that is so practical in hot weather. He himself, Krag, wore an ordinary black suit. A misunderstanding was impossible. Singer had meant Keller.

Keller laughed provocatively.

"You're stunned, aren't you, dear friend?" he said.

"Not at all," replied Krag, "I am only surprised when the expected happens. And this is entirely unexpected."

"I can already see the morning papers," Keller continued in the same teasing tone. "Yesterday, the prisoner gave a complete confession to the capable detective Sirius D. Keller. Also present, Detective Arvid Krag . . . Doesn't that sound fine?", laughed Keller. "This always has a favorable influence on one's chances for promotion. But seriously, Krag, that's just me kidding. I know how much you have put into this investigation. We're in this together and I insist that you come along . . . Why are you staring at me like that?"

Asbjörn Krag was looking at his colleague from top to bottom, eagerly searching, as if he had suddenly discovered something peculiar about him.

"It strikes me for the first time," he said, "how different we both really are. I am tall, thin and sinewy, like a mountaineer, you are of a medium height and muscular, like a sportsman. By the way, the khaki suit looks good on you. You should always wear khaki. At least in this season. The sun is already as strong as if it were the middle of summer."

"What the hell is that supposed to mean?" said Keller, frowning. "Are you making fun of me?"

"Not at all," replied Krag, shaking his head. "I sometimes joke when I'm thinking of something else."

"Are you coming with me or not?"

"Yes, I will accompany you to see whether I will be thrown out."

"By whom?"

"By the prisoner."

"How should a suspect in custody dare to throw you out?"

"If the prisoner says he will not open his mouth while I'm around, it can be said, mildly, that I have been thrown out."

"We will see."

"That's why I am going with you."

Pol got up.

"If I understand correctly," he said, "my expedition is now superfluous."

"On the contrary," said Krag, "it is all the more necessary now."

"Good, then it's time I disappeared."

He took out his wallet, counted the large bills, and grunted in satisfaction.

"Since I am setting out to be robbed," he said, "I wish to be robbed of a decent amount of money. I am nothing if not a man of honor."

Krag went to the window to see Pol leave. Slim and elegant, he slid gracefully into the backseat and the car drove off.

Before the two detectives left for the jail, Krag asked, "Did you read the report about Prison Face?"

"About Georges, yes. And I must confess that I have rarely been so surprised. That doesn't bring us any closer to a solution. The Georges affair is a separate matter, a revenge killing that has nothing to do with the Montrose affair."

"Quite right," replied Krag, "and just such cases make the simplest thing so impenetrable, mysterious. After Georges's confession, I checked his details point-by-point and they all proved to be correct. By the way, when I got the letter from the prison warden, mentioning Charlie's vulgar treachery and Georges's unfortunate experiences, I already had the distinct feeling that Georges had nothing to do with the Montrose affair. By a mere coincidence, the case of Montrose and the case of Georges crossed. If we had assumed that there was an inner connection between these things, we would never have gotten to the bottom of this mystery.

"It is only by accident, we have Charlie's connection with Montrose, because he lived on 28 Hussars Way and was related by marriage to our suspect, Arnold Singer. Georges's revenge might have had another target. If that were the case, this very act of revenge would never have confused our assumptions."

"In the same way," said Keller mischievously, "it might easily happen that other aspects of the investigation will also dissolve into components that have nothing to do with each other. Maybe we're not dealing with one thing here, but with several things that just happened coincidentally."

"I hardly believe that," replied Krag, "because everything else can be attributed directly to the tragic night in Abbot Montrose's garden. By the way, even if Georges's business doesn't concern us directly, his confession explains why Charlie was in such a hurry to get away. He guessed an avenger was on the way. He had to have money to leave that same night. But I'm glad we have sorted out Georges's affair, because it will make the solution of this mess all that much easier."

"Easier," cried Keller, astonished. "By Arnold Singer's confession, hopefully all riddles will be removed."

"Do you think so?" Krag answered. "Well, we'll see what he has to say."

The two detectives got the key from the jailer and stood, a few minutes later, in Arnold Singer's cell.

The two days of his captivity had noticeably changed the gardener. He had grown leaner and his eyes were deep in their sockets. But those eyes still shone with the same calm, intense glow. Krag was still captivated by Singer's gaze, which was penetrating, superior, and alert. Such eyes, thought the detective, belong to a strong-willed and inaccessible man. Just as the previous time, when Krag visited him, and Singer lay stretched out on the cot, his arms crossed under his neck. In front of him on the ground sat a plate of food, which he had not touched.

"Why don't you eat," said Krag.

"Because I'm sick," replied Arnold Singer.

"You have expressed a desire to confess?"

"Yes."

"Why don't you want to do so in front of the court?"

"Because I cannot stand seeing all those silly, curious eyes on me."

"Do you mind if I hear what you have to say?"

"While you are here, I will not say a word. I will only trust one person."

"And you don't want me to be that person?"

"No, I want to confide in this gentleman. What's your name? Keller? Yes. I want to entrust myself to you. It's the only thing left to me, isn't it, to choose the one in whom I want to confide?"

He looked at Krag coldly and dismissively.

"Goodbye, sir," he said.

XXXI. Keller's Papers

"Alright, I'll go," replied Krag, "but will you allow me to confess a certain curiosity. When will you be finished?"

"That depends," answered Arnold Singer, "maybe in an hour, maybe in two. That depends on how long my powers last."

"So, it's a long confession?"

"Yes," answered Arnold Singer, "I will not conceal anything. Everything will come to light, everything, from the first moment. Do you have paper and pencil, Mr. Keller? Good. I want you to write everything down, so that nothing is forgotten."

"Allow me to ask a question," said Krag. "Does your confession also concern the Montrose affair?"

Arnold turned his eyes to him.

"What else?" he asked.

"Will we learn why and how Abbot Montrose disappeared?"

"You will find out," replied Arnold, "how the Abbot died."

"So, he's dead?"

"Yes, irrevocably dead."

Krag stood in front of the prisoner, legs apart, his hands in his sides. He blinked his eyes so strangely, or was it perhaps only his pince-nez, flashing in the light.

"Irrevocably dead," Krag repeated. "That's a strange expression."

"If you knew what I know, you would probably use the same phrase."

"Maybe, maybe," said Krag.

Arnold closed his eyes and waited. Keller also waited feverishly, pencil tip ready on the paper.

Krag turned the key and opened the door.

"Please close the door behind me, Keller," he said.

"Yes," answered Keller.

"Don't forget that the key has to be turned three times."

"Yes, I know," answered Keller and he added, as if reading Krag's thoughts, "besides, I'm here myself."

"Good. Goodbye, gentlemen."

"Goodbye," said Keller.

Arnold said nothing.

When Krag had gone out into the corridor, he waited for a moment, his head bowed thoughtfully, as if considering for a moment before he dared make an important decision. Then he walked slowly down the corridor. In the great hall, where some prison guards walked up and down, he stopped and said, pointing to a flickering gas flame, "You haven't much light here in the evening."

"Of course," said one jailer, stepping toward him, "but if we want to read or write, we'll go to the guardroom."

"Why hasn't the prisoner in 42 been eating?" Krag asked.

"He claims he is ill," answered the guard. "The doctor came to see him today and said he is very weak. He wants to see him again tomorrow."

"But he doesn't have any particular disease?"

"No, nothing definite, general weakness, says the doctor. Malnutrition. I think they spoke about force-feeding."

"I'll talk to the doctor," Krag muttered, and went on. When Krag entered his office, he was still very thoughtful. He stood for a long time at the window and looked over the city, which now lay in blue dusk. The noise of the street was not so loud anymore, the sound of distant church bells could be heard.

Suddenly Krag said to himself—certainly as if he had finally decided, "I'll risk it. . . I'll let him do it. . . "

***

Later in the evening, the police chief asked Asbjörn Krag to come to his office.

His Excellency had the police report on Georges's arrest and confession. The chief was not in a good mood.

"This is a miserable affair," he said. "God knows what the papers will say tomorrow. We have gotten stuck in the Montrose case. Unfortunately, we can't count on the sharp-wittedness of the police to be celebrated in triumph in public opinion tomorrow. The audience is disturbed, the newspapers nervous and abusive. Everyone wants to know something about Montrose, the murderer, or the victim. When I received the news of Georges's arrest last night, I really thought we had sorted this out."

"You went ahead and talked about it among company with the minister?" asked Krag.

His Honor hit the desk with his flat hand.

"I might have mentioned something, yes," he said.

Asbjörn Krag understood that the police chief had spoken prematurely and had informed the high lords that the mystery had already been cleared up. Krag felt sorry for him.

156

"Not a week has passed since the Abbot disappeared, and we've already caught a murderer. I promise you, we'll have the others before the week is over."

"Others? You think they are several?"

Krag shrugged.

"If we knew that with certainty, Excellency," he said, "the case would already be closed."

The police chief got up and nervously walked up and down the room. He crumpled an envelope in his hand.

"In other words, Georges was a worthless catch," he said.

"Not at all," replied the detective. "First, it is always satisfying when a killer is caught, and second, his confession shed some light on a part of the matter, as we now know that Charlie's death is not related to Abbot Montrose's disappearance."

"But other and more dangerous killers still walk free. Understand this. If a new misfortune, a new crime, happens, all our positions are at risk."

"Public opinion is an impatient and unpredictable animal," replied Krag. "But I hope confidently that no new misfortune will upset this beast."

"What do you mean?"

"The work of the police in this matter is not without its dangers," Krag replied, and he was as thoughtful and serious now as he had been a few minutes ago in his own office when he uttered the strange words: "I'll risk it . . . I'll let him do it . . . "

The police chief looked at him, noticed his seriousness and changed his tone. He handed him the letter he had been holding.

"Here's a letter from the Catholic bishop," he said. "He has a message for us."

The letter from the bishop read as follows:

On the occasion of the mysterious disappearance of my friend and fellow believer, Abbot Montrose, it occurred to me that I could provide some enlightenment that may be useful to the investigation. Abbot Montrose wrote a letter to me the evening before the night's drama. This letter doesn't refer to the sad events that took place that night, but perhaps they may matter. I'll be home at twelve o'clock tomorrow.

"What do you think of that?" asked His Excellency.

"You know," replied Krag, "that in the last few days we have received hundreds of messages from people who think they can give us important explanations. Some of them were from friends of the Abbot. None, however, has been able to help us in the least. But, of course, we also want to hear what the bishop has to say. I'll go to him myself."

After Krag had left the police chief, he waited another half hour in his office.

Finally, Keller arrived. He had both hands full of his notes.

Without waiting to see what Keller had to say, Krag led him to a seat under the light and watched him attentively.

"It is true," Krag said, "you are embarrassed and confused. Admit that it was a confession that you had not expected."

Keller leafed through his notes, the paper rustling as if his hands were shaking.

"A very horrible confession," he muttered.

"I've just come from the chief of police," said Krag. "He is impatient because nothing is happening. I could have made him happy if I had told him that Arnold Singer was about to confess. I didn't do it. Did I do the right thing?"

"I really don't know," said Keller uncertainly, "I really don't know— But I know that this is the strangest story of a murder I've ever heard in my practice."

"So, the story of a murder?"

"Yes," said Keller, spreading the papers in front of him.

XXXII. Arnold Singer's Confession—I

Keller, an otherwise sturdy and quiet detective, could not hide the fact that he was as confused as he was upset about what he had heard in prison cell number 42 during the last hour. It so little corresponded with what he expected to hear. He and Asbjörn Krag were alone in the office when he summarized Arnold Singer's confession by reading partly from his notes and partly repeating what he heard from memory. It was in Krag's office where they would be undisturbed; the yellow curtains were drawn. Through the thick walls of the police building, they heard the evening sounds of the city, like roaring waves against a distant shore. The noise was so little they could hear the metallic sound of the gas flames above their heads.

"I have not eaten for several days," began Arnold Singer's confession. "And with extraordinary satisfaction I notice how hunger weakens my physical condition. Gradually, I have been sinking into a dream state that will eventually numb my whole body. Already I feel the heaviness of my limbs. When I raise my arm, because of my fatigue, I notice the weight of the hand, for it involuntarily hangs down at my wrist, and my own fingers appear pale and alien to me. It's as if I've opened my veins and my life force is slowly pouring into a jar. I can already see the moment before me where lack of strength, the complete lack of healthy weight, lends my existence an unusual lightness and levitation.

"It's not a hunger strike, sir, my complete passivity has not occurred because I want to achieve something or protest against something. Apart from my own emotional existence, nothing interests me anymore, I want to bring about a certain state in myself, that's all. I'm about to take stock. I want to seek the deepest motives for my actions, I want to return to the sensations that originally placed my will in these

160

shackles. Now that I am at the end of my reckoning, it no longer satisfies me to conclude that I have acted so and so, or committed these and those misdeeds, no, I am also seeking an answer to the always-dreadful 'why?', the inexorable and sphinxlike question that pursues the life of unfortunates. I believe that the answer will finally reach me, not in the form of words or direct manifestations, but as a faint but convincing sensation and hunch; I'll certainly experience an understanding that will come to me from the outer limits of existence like a piercing breeze. I am preparing my mind. I want to push myself to the limit of human dissolution so that my mind becomes free and receptive. I have chosen the agony of hunger.

"There are other pathways that lead to the strange unreality where the soul captures hunches, revelations, smells, sounds that otherwise cannot reach us. We have the path of fever, where the soul is torn from the body, leaving it clear-eyed and highly receptive to all indefinite impressions as it flows toward the dark regions of death. We also have the path of the terrible cold. But I chose hunger.

"I wanted to be alone with you, not because you are dearer to me than someone else, but because your everyday appearance looks soothing to me. Your presence is welcome to me so that I am not forced to speak in soliloquy, which would only result in my own voice irritating me. So, I am about to confess, and I want to do so in a state of mind and in a form that at the same time satisfies my curiosity about myself. For it's not only to the police that a criminal is a mystery, he is often a mystery to himself. Freed from the material labors of life, I want to look critically at my own actions, while my ability to think is visionary but clear; like a man who, facing death, lives through all the events of his life in a few minutes. I'll try to understand my innermost motives. That's why I cannot put my confession to murder in front of the courtroom. I no longer see the factual structure of the murder. Already in its visionary state, my mind has dismissed the very soul of the murder, the trembling fright that precedes the deed, the unspeakable anxiety of the moment, the dreadful subsequent silence.

"How clearly do I remember everything when I close my eyes . . . oh, that scent of spring and apple blossom; it was in the spring when it happened.

161

"Imagine a house," continued Arnold Singer's strange confession, "imagine an ordinary house of yellow sandstone. It is located in the outskirts of a small city and it is an evening in late May. I shall describe the surroundings later, because at the moment I feel nothing other than the mood that the stillness of the evening aroused in me, the trees that flanked the villa, immovable and towering, the air of the deepened spring brisk at the edge of the sky, green and clear like Rhine wine. The sun has set in the west, but still its brilliance rests on the upper branches of the trees. As I stood and waited, I could follow the waning day in the changing play of light on the treetops. Like a golden, glittering cobweb, the rays caught in the foliage, where they formed wondrous, coppery grottos. Almost imperceptibly, the strip of light lifted, finally to depart from the topmost branches. The garden became darker. The dusk settled on the trees and the foliage shook in the cooling air, or was it only my heart that quaked in fear and premonition?

"Is there anything more peaceful than such a small house at the edge of the city, on the border with the countryside with fields and forests? More modest but more honest than a house in a big city, it expresses the peaceful pursuits of everyday life. During the day, it is sunlit and warm, with white, friendly curtains that flutter in the open windows. A lady in a light summer dress comes slowly and carelessly humming to herself, down the stairs to cut some beautiful flowers in the garden. A child plays with a dog. A man takes a seat on the balcony in the shade of a red and white striped awning and unfolds a newspaper. Muffled piano sounds from inside the house, snatches of everyday words that can clearly be heard on the dusty white country road, the highway itself, with the tracks of bicycles and milk trucks, the smoke rising from the chimney, the telephone wires entering the yellow wall, the fence around the garden with its even stakes and the elaborate gate, the sound of footfall on the stone steps, the sound of the noonday bell ringing through the open windows, all this—is it not an expression of the peaceful life of ordinary people, eternal and unshakeable, which is called family, day by day, year by year? . . . Then when evening comes, the people in the house go to bed. The windows darken and the whole house gets that sleeping look that houses tend to have on quiet summer nights when they rest in their own dull shadows. A dog barks, a cat pads past, and the house sleeps in undisturbed peace. Such a house can be seen from the outside as holding untroubled people, people whose hearts are not beating faster in fear of some danger. Suddenly, one night, when everything is quiet, the house silently changes its appearance. How such black windows can suddenly look terrified when a killer comes out from the shadow of the tallest tree and climbs over the fence. The murderer, sir, who is no longer a human being, but just a being, far from all the innocence of the child in which all human horror and the primitive terror of all times are united."

XXXIII. Arnold Singer's Confession—II

"What did I say? Has he already climbed over the fence? My thoughts have preceded the events, sir. I feel the same tremor, the same restlessness as then. Even then, my imagination preceded the events. I was within a wave of frightened expectation. I tried to drown my fear in the unbearable rush of the moment. So, it is again now, when I try to recall all the details in my memory; my heart is pounding wild, faster! faster! Like an animal who smells food, I rush to a decision, to the irrevocable decision that will calm my mind. And yet I now realize that on my journey from the garden fence to the oak front door, I have experienced an infinity of observations and moods. A journey, I call it, sir, though it is only a brief walk of a few minutes. In these few minutes but just before the event, the killer travels a strange journey under the skies of his own changing moods. All his senses are open with an unheard-of susceptibility, everything he hears and sees, everything he experiences, every trifle acquires an unusual meaning, while the violent impulses in his nerves drive him forward. Time itself has changed its pace. That's why he feels the seconds as heavy, his sense of perception works in the most heightened way, a shadow, a leaf in his path, the sound of a rolling stone, become great, momentous events that cause fright, reflection, despair, and again, determination. Oh, sir, it is true that a killer is the greatest enemy of life. So, all the manifestations of life join to make his final steps a long, dreadful journey. If he overcomes them, then he accomplishes his goal, but he is always caught by the painful eternity of these last minutes.

"What does the killer see as he slides over the fence in the shadow of the tallest tree?

"He sees the house sleeping in silence. The trees are dark, the road has become gray. The landscape rests in the night like a half-smeared

164

charcoal drawing, only the tall poplars show their contours, like two black cracks in the deep blue bowl of the sky; as he steps under a tree and touches its foliage, he thinks that the rustling leaves sound like a whisper from the branches. In the silence that follows, it is as if the tree has said something aloud and as if the whole garden breathlessly listens to its terrible message. A bat flies past the killer on inaudible wings. His soul quivers. He feels as if it is flying through his heart. A cobweb thread cuts razor-sharp across his forehead, and the sound of the softly crackling gravel beneath his feet touches him with a cold icy chill. The grass is wet with dew and sticks to the soles of his shoes like a blood-saturated carpet. Myriad moths swarm around him, he doesn't see them, but feels their wingbeats against his eyelids and captures with an unspeakably sensitive ear the sharpest and quietest sound of the night: a silvery rush of the legions of molecules. The air is filled with living things. Nearby there is a pond. He imagines he is wading in the pond, the dark lawns under the trees are like reeds in still water. Seized by a sudden and unmotivated idea, he anxiously looks for a dead man lying quietly moonlit in the reeds; the moon, however, doesn't show itself tonight, and what he sees is grass, ice-green turfs, shaped like graves, and above the trees he sees shuddering the airy drapery of the Milky Way. Has one second passed in the eternity of the murderer?

"He comes to an open place and stops involuntarily because he is no longer protected from the deep shadows and the immediate vicinity of the trees. The branches, which he has bent aside during his stealthy hike, glide back into their original positions and once again everything becomes quiet. The open space around him becomes cold and hostile, and he feels seized by the almost irresistible desire to hide. He senses that he is in the line of danger and that he can be hit the next moment. Hit by what? It would reassure him if he sensed the slightest manifestation of human life, just a distant voice or a step on the path. But this uninterruptedly observant and mute natural landscape has an unbelievably oppressive effect on him. The stone posts of the gate have their granite gaze focused on him. The unfathomable masses of poplars hide eyes that he cannot see, but whose alert and threatening power he feels. Everything human in him has given way to the evil soul of the murderer and it now populates the dead things around him with haunting reproaches; his conscience stares at him from the gray brightness of the highway. Fearfully, he looks up at the house, and suddenly realizes that the house has discovered him and is expecting his arrival. The house has wrenched open its black window eyes! Human eyes cannot express a more intense shock than these maliciously staring black caves.

"He sees only the upper three square, black windows; the lower ones are hidden from the garden. He also vaguely sees the rolled-up awnings over the window frames, which reinforce the resemblance to opened and startled eyes. As the killer stares at this phantom, this dream-like face of stone and shadow, his own ever-changing, presumptuous frame-of-mind takes on a new form. He thinks he sees his own fear in the phantom house. Slowly, as if one photograph is projected over another, a new image enters his wide-open eyes. The trees in front of the house, between the branches of which the murderer saw the bright and friendly curtains of the window in the evening, and a woman leaning carelessly against the window frame—these trees now stand like dark abysses on either side of the stairs. Something has suddenly fallen away from the face of the house and disappeared, the darkness of the trees forming two huge, empty eye sockets, and the bone-yellow stone of the façade is like the silhouette of a skull against the night sky. So, all the senses of death and demise fulfilled, he goes to murder, even the air sweats out a pervasive smell of cemetery. Bats flutter around him on black, silent wings. With every creeping step in the damp grass he summons the spirits of murder, these beings of darkness and silence. Now they are hovering above his head, silently, in rising and falling flight . . .

"Where have I been? I feel like I'm not following him anymore, and yet I am the killer. I stand outside in the garden, surrounded by an indescribable spring fragrance. And yet I find myself in front of the panel door with its broad, brown-stained boards. What am I waiting for out here? Now it comes. At the death cry of the victim, I tell you, sir, not only the victim screams. In this cry, all the mute figures grow eloquent. The impotent horror of the home, the watchful darkness of the poplars, all that belongs to man and his friends, the stone pillars of the gate, the country road, the mowed grass of the lawn, all that have seen with inhuman, watchful eyes the arrival of the murderer, all vent their pain in the death cry of the victim, as an everlasting indictment of everything that belongs to life and man. Then the murderer hears the cry, yes, I heard it—"

Keller has finished. As he read, he had been running his hand over his hair. Now he could think of nothing better to do than nervously leaf through the papers, his fingers trembling, he was very nervous and looked up questioningly.

"My goodness," cried Krag astonished, "is that all?"

"Yes, until further notice. When he got that far, he closed his eyes and said he was dead tired. I should come back in a few hours, then he would go on."

"Are you taking notes? Is that exactly what he said?"

"No. I memorized it and I'm going to take it on stage as a cabaret act. Yes, of course I'm taking notes."

"Alright, fine. And what do you believe?" Krag asked.

"What I believe," Keller said with a bitter smile, "I think you doubt."

"I don't mean that. What do you think of the confession?"

Keller, the otherwise cool detective, was obviously greatly shaken by his experience with Arnold Singer. He eagerly shared what a strong impression this man had made on him.

"He seems to be a very strange phenomenon in the life of the big city," he said. "I'm sure we can expect the strangest revelations from him. He is a product of our overripe civilization. You know, dear Krag, that during the last two or three years several mysterious murders have remained unsolved. Imagine if Arnold Singer would solve these secrets for us. Maybe he's some sort of mystical figure, one of the weird predators of big city life – a serial killer."

"But Montrose?" Krag asked, laughing.

"Yes, Montrose—that'll come, that'll come later. I also asked him about Montrose. 'That is coming,' he said. It will take another hour for the interrogation to begin again. I've rarely been so excited."

"I just want to remind you," said Krag, putting on his coat, "I just want to remind you of what we must learn above all, namely, where is Montrose? Is he dead or alive?

"Who and where are his murderers or those who kidnapped him?

"Where are the men who murdered the mad professor?"

"I believe," said Keller, "that Arnold Singer murdered Abbot Montrose."

"But, dear friend, can one rely on his reason when he says so? He is very abstracted and otherworldly right now."

"His otherworldliness gives him a visionary memory of everything that has happened. You should have seen his face when I left him and before I put out the light. He was petrified, absent . . . I can't get it out of my mind."

Krag also thought about him. He imagined him motionless in the dark cell. But not motionless. Now Arnold Singer traveled in a hollow cube of stone, far from everything present, towards the crimes of earlier days and the horrors of formerly experienced hours.

That's what Asbjörn Krag thought about.

XXXIV. Dora

That evening the Peacock was crowded with people. The sensation of Abbot Montrose's disappearance and the scandalous murder in the hotel itself had become a huge advertisement for the bar. Three times the doors had to be closed, so large was the influx of curious guests. The Raincloud, who had resumed his residence behind the bar in his red and white abundance, didn't like this crowd at all, because he understood the cause very well. The curious, who naively asked if they could see the room where the professor had been murdered, received a terrible look from the swollen eyes of the Raincloud and a hoarse, growling sound whose significance only Rudolf grasped. The understanding waiter hurried to bring the obtrusive questioners out to the street for their own safety.

"Go away, gentlemen, disappear . . . for God's sake. He only hums once. Then it comes."

"What happens then?" asked the uprooted patrons, disgruntled.

Rudolf sculpted the air with vivid gestures to show what would come when the Raincloud grunted again. And this sculpture was so clear in master Rudolf's presentation that the curious ones fell silent. It was therefore not advisable to approach the Raincloud today. His bad temper also weighed on his surroundings, the beautiful ladies in their white clouds of tulle and powder that flanked his mighty corpus. This despondency in the cloudy realm, however, gave rise to a more intimate exchange of ideas. The young gentleman with the golden chain was also present that evening. He was quite happy, because instead of swarming around and chatting with the guests, his chosen one sat quietly and neatly with her crochet hook. As she sat there so domestically with downcast eyes, she might have been a virtuous

169

noblewoman of yesteryear. The young man still didn't say a word, but just stared at her and occasionally sipped at his small, green glass having not yet crossed to the stage of unhappy, unrequited love. The only one who was a bit disturbing was Dora, as usual. You could see from her glistening eyes that she had already been busy with the bottles. She was far from her peak inebriation, when she would lead the revelries in the gallant Peacock with her coppery hair and shrill voice. The other girls vented their restlessness by exchanging tins of face powder, smelling each other's perfume, and carefully polishing their nails and hand mirrors. And the Raincloud rumbled.

But for the one whose intent was to intervene in the throng this evening, this crowd was excellent and welcome. There were so many strange faces there that none of them attracted attention. Even the keenest observer could discover nothing but the arrival of curious onlookers and their obvious excitement over the eerie recent events. And yet, there was something in the crowd, something definite, something that was accompanied by mysterious winks, sly signs, and hasty whispers in passing. A middle-aged man, with a hard, unpleasant face, came through the door of the hotel. He stood for a while, unaffected by the crowd, peering, watching. Then, with sudden energy, he sat down on a stool in front of the bar and ordered a drink. He arrived just as Dora allowed herself an exuberant salvo of laughter. She paused in the midst of it and looked at him, but then began laughing, if possible, even louder. There was no sign of recognition on her face. No one greeted him or even acknowledged his presence. He was a stranger. A man with short, coal-black hair that dropped onto his forehead in a thick curl, unknown, unremarked, unseen.

Why was Dora laughing? Poor Dora had to keep up her reputation of being the most cheerful among the cheerful—she usually laughed for any reason. But in her half-drunken exaltation, she was prone to laugh for no reason at all. All this was in an effort to prove to the Raincloud that, as far as gaiety was concerned, she had no equal. This time, however, she really had cause for her exuberance. The little viscount, Pol, the darling of all the girls in all the cabarets in the city, had returned; he had been gone an hour and now he was back and far more drunk than Dora herself.

Pol and Dora sat at a polished marble table and put their heads together. Pol, who had just returned from a private – and unlicensed – gaming club, was a talkative drunk and began to chatter.

"First, I bet a hundred," he said, "and lost. So, I bet two hundred and lost. So, I bet three hundred and lost. Then I bet one thousand and won, bravo! Then I set another thousand . . . and won again. Then I bet only a hundred and lost two hundred. Lost. So, I bet a thousand and won, bravo!"

Dora laughed unusually loudly.

"Let me see," she said.

Pol pulled a handful of bills and gold out of his pocket. Dora yelled for champagne. Two champagne corks popped. Pol drank and spilled most of it on the marble table. Dora drank and spilled more, whereupon she accidentally made one bottle disappear under the table and ordered two new bottles with increasing cheerfulness.

And Pol told her, "I won consistently. Then came the owner, a very fine gentleman, Whiskers like an English lord, a gold watch, a coat of arms on one pocket, a marked card game in the other. Hmm, hmm. 'I'm glad to see your luck in the card games,' said the proprietor, 'a glass, sir.' 'No, thank you,' I said, 'but a cigar that will not allow me to be stunned or poisoned,' I said. Then I bet a thousand and won. The proprietor cried, not tears, but whiskey. Then came ladies, beautiful ladies, bravo. 'Give me a little of your profit,' Leonora said, you know her certainly. 'Two,' I said, 'two bills,' and then I stuffed them in her waistband, you know, here, tentatively, don't cry so terribly, Dora . . ."

But she squealed overjoyed and kept the bills, and she put Pol's hand on her breast.

Poor Pol, meanwhile, became more and more drunk, once he even fell asleep, his head on the marble plate. But he was relentlessly awakened by Dora, who knocked him on the head. When he raised his head again, he had reached the elegiac stage, he had tears in his eyes and whispered his passionate love to Dora. While he tried, in vain, to fall from the chair to his knees, Dora stealthily exchanged glances with the unsympathetic stranger. He was lighting a cigar; his eyes were half-hidden, cold and commanding behind his cigar smoke.

Neither these secret signs, nor Pol's unfortunate drunkenness or Dora's cheerfulness had caught anyone's attention. Such performances were much too commonplace in the Peacock, besides, the place was swarming with people, so that it was not possible to understand a word in all the noise. The man with the black curl on his forehead paid and left and a new guest took his place.

It was an elderly gentleman, one of those types often seen in such places, the sad ruins of former bon vivants. His cheeks were rouged, with a few strands of hair over his forehead, like hollow straws of hay, and when he moved, his gouty limbs crackled audibly. A lifetime of dissipation expressed itself in a lack of eloquence remarkable in one so well-dressed. But he was delighted by the presence of the beautiful women and he ceaselessly adjusted his pince-nez to see better behind the counter. And when he thought he had discovered something amusing, he said, "Er . . . er . . . er . . ." and laughed.

This older bon vivant took Pol's place as the intoxicated player staggered out of the restaurant after a whispered conversation with Dora.

The cheerful and robust Dora had apparently completely turned his head.

The marble table looked sad after Pol's excesses.

"Ew," said the older gentleman.

At the same time, he placed the flat of his hand on the edge of the table, and there he left it.

In the marble, some almost invisible signs were engraved, and these signs were covered by the older gentleman's hand.

"Room 32. Here."

Pol had scratched it with his diamond ring.

XXXV. Pol Sobers Up

Head bowed, hair hanging over his forehead like a curtain, the intoxicated Pol swayed out of the bar. He had arranged a rendezvous with Dora in Room 32. First, he had agreed with her that he would pick her up in a car and drive to another nightclub where they could continue their drinking, but suddenly she had changed her mind and whispered to him, "Room 32, the stairs on the left." Maybe she found him too drunk and preferred to be alone with him in a room. However, Dora was not like that. She was always drunk herself and enjoyed drunken suitors with gold in their pockets. Besides, her change of mind had come suddenly. Had she received a signal? Pol remembered the unpleasant man with the brutal face and the scar on one cheek, the clear, cold, scrutinizing eyes, and the black curl on his forehead. "If this man was in touch with Dora, I must be careful," Pol thought, and made sure he had his revolver in his pocket. Yes, it was there. And he thought about it as he had climbed the stairs.

Now one can rightly ask how an intoxicated man like Pol was capable of such thoughtfulness. From all that happened on that memorable evening, however, it appears that the viscount was by no means as intoxicated as he would like to appear.

Pol had been downstairs several times in the bar and joked with the girls, but he had never set foot in the hotel. That is why the strange decorations on the walls astonished him. Where the restaurant was full of restless energy, the hotel was very quiet. The narrow, half-dark, carpet-covered corridors that crossed each other like catacombs breathed their own mysterious moods. He thought of all the people who lived here, Asians, Americans, and Europeans, blacks and whites, characters from the hubbub of the art world—and he had an inkling that this hotel, with its many rooms, was home to the strangest

173

mysteries. Then he heard a felt-covered door open carefully near him, and, believing himself watched, he fell back into his almost senseless intoxicated state. With a dragging step, pushing against the walls, he wandered through the corridors and looked for the door numbers. The irregular order of numbers confused him so much that for a moment he really believed he was drunk. Finally, by a mere coincidence, he found Room 32.

Pol had studied the forms of drunkenness in all its nuances. No seasoned actor could play a drunk better than he could. In a way, he enjoyed his role and completed it with all the bits and pieces of involuntary comedy that the alcohol-charged man does best. Just listen to him banging on the door. First restless and almost inaudible, as if he had miscalculated the distance and barely touched the door with his fingers. But then, when he wanted to knock more certainly, two terrible blows against the door, so that it shivered in its lock. He repeated this maneuver several times, then without waiting for an answer, wrenched open the door and staggered into the room, his hand sticking to the doorknob as though glued to it. He then got involved in the extensive business of closing the door, almost stumbling back into the corridor. Finally, he was happily in the room with the door closed. The room was empty. Pol stopped for a few moments and looked around. He immediately discovered that the bed was in an alcove and was covered by a curtain. Therefore, he continued in the role of the drunk and slipped into an armchair, where he remained sitting bent over. And, so, several minutes passed.

At last the curtain parted, a man stepped out and stood in front of Pol.

It was the man from the bar with the black curl.

He stood for a while, looking at Pol.

Pol raised his heavy head and looked at him with blurry eyes.

Then the stranger said, "How long are you planning to play this comic role?"

"Where is Dora?" Pol slurred.

"Stop it," answered the stranger. "You are not drunk at all. I've watched you all evening."

"I want a bottle of dry champagne. And then I want to have a bottle of sweet champagne. Hah! I've won thousands . . . several thousands, bravo!"

The stranger went to the door and locked it.

Pol got up hastily and staggered between the chair and the table. He tried to hold on to the corner of the table, which only meant that a flower vase fell over.

"What kind of an insolent rogue are you?" Pol asked. "Are you married to Dora, eh?"

Whereupon he sank back into the chair and pulled the tablecloth with him.

The stranger took up his position again in front of Pol.

"We have very little time," he said.

"We," cried Pol, as if with a glimmer of reason, "We! Go to hell, I have plenty of time. I don't need to be in my office until 19 . . . 24."

The long year caused him difficulties, but finally he managed to get it out.

"It's a pity about your talent," said the stranger, laughing scornfully, "you should have been an actor. You might even have succeeded in deceiving me if I had not been watching you for several hours. You can stop now."

But Pol was not so easily frightened. He kept saying foolish things about Dora and champagne.

Then the stranger called, "Harry!"

A new figure emerged from behind the bed curtain, a stocky man in sailor's clothing holding a rubber truncheon in his hand.

"There you see my friend Harry," said the stranger almost cheerfully. "Notice what he holds in his hand and notice his strong arms. Can you see how much that club wants to meet you? See? It's already wagging its tail. Hello, no, keep your hand out of your pocket! One more move and it's over for you. Take the little pistol from him, Harry. Look, a pretty little gun, D Coll model 1910—a police revolver, I thought so. Let's talk seriously now, it's high time. We have to negotiate a very important matter, my dear sir."

Pol straightened up.

"Sit down," he said, "I don't like talking to standing people when I'm sitting myself."

"Well, that's another tone," said the stranger, sitting down at the table opposite Pol. He played jokingly with Pol's revolver, and Pol kept his eyes on his fingers. The stranger seemed to guess his thoughts.

"No," he said, "no, you have nothing to fear. We don't use such noisy toys. Why should we disturb the happy people down there in their pleasure? On the other hand, you must not forget my friend Harry with the club. As you may be kind enough to notice, he is standing behind you. He's just waiting for a hint from me. Whether I give him that hint is entirely up to you."

"Where did you learn such educated language, Toby?" Pol asked.

"My name isn't Toby."

"Well, then Tommy or any other name from the harbor. You must have been an elevator boy or something, and you were fired because the travelers' pockets were not safe from your fingers."

"Harry," the stranger said gently, "dear Harry—"

Pol laughed.

"You didn't lure me here to kill me," he said. "I suppose I'll keep my senses until I find out what you want from me. Now, gentlemen, my dear villains, I beg you to hurry, I have pressing appointments."

176

"What we wish can be said in a few words," said the stranger, "we want you to write a letter."

"And if I refuse?"

"That is unthinkable," answered the other, laughing. "You will write this letter."

Pol watched his expression and privately admitted to himself that he might indeed be taking up correspondence.

XXXVI. Pol's Letter

Although the viscount quietly admitted to himself that danger was imminent, his appearance betrayed nothing. On the contrary. He was not clear about the thugs' intentions and it was rather doubtful how the adventure would go. But he was presented with a new sensation tickling his nerves, and that was why he was basically very happy, which he showed by good humor. All he needed was a cup of coffee, or a glass of wine, to make it appear that he was sitting in a salon talking about the most indifferent things in the world. His indifferent appearance irritated the others.

"I imagine," he said, "that none of these gentlemen thieves can write a letter. Of course, a man with such a curl as yours, Tommy, cannot spell correctly . . . orthographically. If I should write a letter for you, addressed to the love of your life, and you can be sure that no one understands how to express such genuine feelings in a letter as I do. Why, just yesterday I wrote a letter for my cook to her soldier. 'Beloved Roland,' that's how I started . . . No, no, my dear Harry, don't wave the club so hard through the air. It could hit me, and an unconscious man cannot write. So, my lords of the scum, if it's a love letter, I'm ready. I just don't understand why you need to create so much inconvenience for a very ordinary love letter to your cook. I would also have been at your service for less. Is she called Kathinka? Is she very beautiful? Is she very popular, my dear Tommy? Are you delighted to think about her beauty? Bravo! Or are you only showing your teeth?"

"One minute," Tommy said, placing his watch on the table in front of him.

"How popular is she?" asked Pol, "What do you mean?"

"In a minute you will shut your mouth," answered the man with the curl, and, glancing at his comrade, he added, "Did you understand, Harry?"

"Yes, of course," answered Harry, swinging the club to and fro to get it going.

Pol pointed his finger at the clock.

"One minute," he cried, "excellent. I'm not in the mood, gentlemen, I regret that, because you have no idea what I can say in the course of a minute. The knife scar on your neck, you black-haired boar, I see that you've been in combat with an honorable man you probably wanted to rob. Your rotted heart stinks through your breath, you bastard orphan. Your horribly long fingers are dirty from the linings of other people's pockets. Your eyes are squinting intensely because, for once, you are not hiding in the dark waiting for an ambush. Your feet, shoved into the boots that you stole from a poor shoemaker with seven abandoned children, seem to have been used mainly to kick others. If your whore of a mother had any decency, you would have been drowned at birth like the mangy dog you are. If there were any justice in the world, I would be writing a letter to my friend at the police station, 'Here I am sitting with two scoundrels, hold a gallows in readiness, and inform the senior physician at the hospital that a pair of carcasses will arrive soon.'"

"Stop!"

Pol raised his forefinger.

"Two seconds," he called. "Now I'll shut up, gentlemen. Let's hear your proposal."

Whereupon he pressed his lips together and crossed his arms.

The revolver shook in the hand of the criminal, who was trembling with rage. Pol watched him curiously and thought, "If he shakes too hard, the gun may easily fire." The criminal laughed. But it was a strange laugh. And Pol was right when he asked, "Are you laughing or baring your teeth?"

Harry, however, Harry with the club was completely agape at Pol's impudence and quite impressed with his stock of curses. First, he looked at Pol, who sat there completely untouched, swinging his patent-leather shoe up and down in front of his comrade's nose. Then he looked at his comrade with boundless astonishment, as if to say, "Why is this cur still alive?"

Aloud he said, "Time flies, Bussi."

So Bussi was the nickname of the man with the curl, thought Pol.

Bussi put the revolver on the table.

"I have to say that you have an excellent vocabulary. But as far as the letter is concerned, we seem quite in agreement."

"Really, I'm glad."

"Yes, I accept your suggestion that you write a letter to your friend at the police station."

"Whereupon I immediately withdraw my suggestion," said Pol.

Bussi stamped his foot angrily. "You want to gain time with your accursed chatter," he said, "but you will not succeed. Listen to what I require of you. I want you to write a letter to a man at the police station. Will you do it? Yes or no?"

"I have no ink," said Pol.

"Yes or no!"

"Yes, hell. Have a little patience, man."

"You have delayed me long enough," Bussi shouted angrily. "Get the ink bottle from over there, Harry. So here you have ink. There's paper."

"But I have no quill," said Pol.

Harry threw a quill on the table and used the opportunity to hold a hairy and threatening fist under Pol's nose.

Pol turned the page back and forth. "Should I start on this side of the paper or would you rather on the other side?" he asked.

"Harry," said the man with the curl, "give him a reminder."

Harry swung the club.

"Stop," shouted Pol, "don't touch me, you can't beat a man holding a quill in his hand."

This strange assertion stopped Harry in his tracks.

Pol was holding the quill ready. He looked up questioningly at Bussi.

"Write," said Bussi. "Dear Krag."

Pol whistled through his teeth.

"Write!" howled Bussi.

"Just allow me one remark," said Pol docilely. "Although I am not a pickpocket, not even destined for the gallows, I still have a certain courtesy. Allow me to write to dear *Mr.* Krag."

"Hell, write what you want. So, 'Dear Mr. Krag,' Are you finished?"

"'Dear Mr. Krag'—continue."

"Come immediately and unnoticed to Room 32 and tell no one, the Gilded Peacock Hotel. Come in complete secrecy. Tap the door three times. I am waiting for you."

"Hello," said Bussi suddenly, reaching for his revolver, "Who's there?"

There had been a knock on the door, three long and three short blows.

"That's Dora's signal," Bussi said. "Open it, Harry."

181

Harry opened the door.

It was Mr. Krag. Mr. Asbjörn Krag.

XXXVII. The Fairytale Is Over

Krag had calculated correctly. He knew that his unexpected arrival would be so startling to the circle that he would win the few seconds he needed. He also anticipated Pol's presence of mind. And, on the whole, he was not mistaken. No sooner had he come through the door than he was standing in front of Bussi with his revolver raised. Bussi backed away from the table to seize Pol's revolver. But Pol had already taken it and was holding Harry in check. The two criminals had lost those precious seconds, and the two detectives were now superior to them. Nonetheless, the situation was dangerous, and it could easily become critical if the criminals became desperate. Bussi's eyes flickered, searching for a way out.

"I need to talk to you," said Krag. "Don't do anything imprudent, because at the slightest movement I will shoot. We are not alone, either."

"Hello," he suddenly called loudly, "are you outside, Keller?"

"Yes," answered a rough man's voice from the corridor, "and there are four of us."

"And under the window?"

"Four more there, too," answered the voice, "all the escapes are covered."

Bussi spat a curse.

"So, you see," said Krag, "that any resistance is in vain. Hands up, gentlemen, that's it! And throw away the club, friend, you have no use for it anymore. That's nice. Now it's your turn, Pol, be so kind as to examine the men's pockets. I think we will find some nice things there. A revolver, look, another one, hmm, you are terribly well armed, my dear Bussi. And what about Harry? Another revolver! And a dagger, eh, that's a barbarian weapon, dear friend, one, if I may say so, unfriendly weapon, which, however, has the merit of being silent. Meanwhile I prefer fists. Right, put everything there on the dresser, Pol, it's a whole arsenal, and would you take now from my left pocket a pair of shiny cuffs, which I brought with me. That's right, in this pocket. I am sure you know how to use those things, Pol. Yes, excellent; and then the other, crack, crack, yes, this lock is a bit heavy. Thank you. Now they are both nicely decorated. And if I may ask the gentlemen now to take a seat. Don't look so angry, Bussi, sit down! I say. I am a polite but also a very determined man."

Reluctantly, the two criminals sat. As they sat there handcuffed, they looked defiant and gloomy.

Krag lowered his revolver.

"It was about time," he said, "my arm was getting very stiff."

Pol picked up the club from the ground and whipped it back and forth.

"It was after me," said the viscount, laughing, "but I fooled it."

Harry looked at him spitefully and stealthily. Pol swung the club in front of his nose.

"Would you like to hold a quill in your hand?" Pol asked Harry. "I'm told that you can't beat a man holding a quill."

Krag read the letter Pol had just written.

"This is an invitation," he said. "Thank you, gentlemen, but I prefer to surprise such hosts as yourselves with an unannounced visit. Incidentally, I see through your intentions, and am very sad about the decline of noble hospitality, about which I need not speak further. What was waiting for me? Probably being hit with that bludgeon as soon as I entered the room. Maybe something worse. I was becoming a bit difficult for these gentlemen. They discovered that I was on their trail and that's why it was important to get rid of me. I must confess, you act quickly and ruthlessly. When a few days ago it was time to get rid of another burdensome man, namely, Strantz, the Crazy Professor, he too was promptly delivered to the afterlife. Just in front of our noses, but something like that doesn't repeat itself, gentlemen. The event taught us caution. You also have other sins on your conscience; you have run up a long and unpleasant bill and it's waiting to be paid, but we had lost your trail for a while. It is wise to disappear now and then, eh, Gentlemen? How did you like it aboard the schooner *Eddystone*, Bussi, good, right? Next time, however, don't leave a scarf in such bright Spanish colors. You make it too easy. And now, we come to the main thing. Yes, you also must be responsible for the pretty little affair in Abbot Montrose's garden."

"That damn priest," grunted Bussi, "he spoiled everything."

"Where is he?" Pol asked.

Bussi didn't answer.

"What did he say to you?" asked Krag.

"Nothing. But he must know where the priest is," replied Pol.

"If I knew that," said Bussi, "I would have killed him long ago."

"Nice pair," muttered Krag. "Good that we've got them arrested now."

Krag went to the window and looked out.

"Quite right," he said as if to himself, "this is an excellent room. Enter through the door, out through the window, or vice versa. I think I'll have to get the police to close this hotel. The Raincloud is too old and too thick to keep the guests in check. We cannot have such a rat's nest for criminals in the middle of the city."

Krag went through the room and opened the door.

"But where is everyone?" he exclaimed.

The corridor outside was empty. Bussi muttered some indistinct but angry words between his teeth.

Krag closed the door again and began to laugh.

"There are no men outside," he said, "nor under the window. I am an excellent ventriloquist and it's not the first time that my talent has helped me out of trouble. You become more numerous, so to speak, when you are alone."

Krag stopped in front of the handcuffed criminal and said, "Admit that the fairy tale is over, my dear Hans Christian Andersen." The criminal jumped.

"Yes, I recognize you," continued Krag in his most amiable tone, pouring water into the basin to wash away the rouged traces of the old bon vivant with the hay-colored hair from his face. "Besides, it doesn't mean anything if you're of Danish descent. I think that your parents wanted to use that name to express the great hope they put in you. You should also climb high, my dear Hans Christian Andersen, with the nom de guerre Bussi. I promise you that you will be elevated. But you will also fall deeply. How deep is the fall? At least six feet, I've been told . . . Ah, it's soothing to get rid of the mask. I don't love playing such old gentlemen, but I was forced to do so. The girls looked at me with disgust, even Dora. Poor Dora, she won't be laughing about this. However, I hope that she will prove to be a relatively innocent employee. Her unnatural cheerfulness has something appealing. Now I hear by the heavy footsteps on the stairs that our people really are coming, Pol, I hereby give you the supreme command. Make sure that our guests receive safe, but sound accommodations. Farewell, gentlemen, we'll meet again in another and larger hall."

It was four o'clock in the morning before Krag returned to the guard room. He asked for Keller.

"Keller left two hours ago," one of the attending police officers replied, "and has not returned yet."

"Two hours ahead, then," said Krag.

186

The police officer was startled.

"What do you mean?" He exclaimed.

"I only mean," replied Krag, "that the mystery of Montrose no longer exists, the riddle is solved. Come on, follow me to Arnold Singer's cell."

XXXVIII. His Eminence

It was a quiet night at the police station. There were a few police officers in the guardroom. On the way to the cell, Asbjörn Krag stopped in the dark corridor and asked one of the police guards, "How long have you been on duty?"

"From eight to twelve o'clock and from two to now."

"So, you saw Detective Keller pass by here?"

"Yes, several times. He paid Arnold Singer several long visits. The last time he left immediately after I resumed my watch. Keller went past here and out the door to the left."

"How was he dressed?" Krag asked.

"Dressed?" The policeman didn't seem to understand. "He was wearing his khaki suit," he said.

The policeman that Krag had first met in the guardroom told him that at about one o'clock in the morning he had exchanged a few words with Keller. Keller had been greatly moved by his visits to Arnold Singer. He had made his second visit to the prisoner and wanted to return to him as soon as the sick and exhausted man had rested for an hour. Keller had said something about unrelated revelations, psychological riddles, strange types of criminals, and the like, and had been very upset about it all.

Krag listened to these messages on the way to Arnold Singer's cell without it seeming to interest him. He was completely absorbed in his own thoughts. The guards who accompanied him heard him say to himself in a low voice, "Maybe I should not have risked it . . . well, we can only hope for the best."

They stopped at the door of Arnold Singer's cell.

Krag grabbed the door handle.

"The door is locked," he said.

The jailer laughed.

"Yes, of course it's locked," he said, "I'm sure Keller was careful to lock it up behind him."

"Unlock it," said Krag.

The jailer rattled the keys.

"The poor sick prisoner is certainly tired now," he said. "Couldn't you wait until tomorrow?"

"Unlock it," Krag said again.

When the door was opened, and the police entered the narrow cell, they encountered an unexpected sight. In the pale morning light streaming in through the window, they saw a half-dressed man lying as if dead on the floor.

Krag hurried toward him and bent over him as the others backed away and stopped petrified.

After a hasty examination Krag straightened up. His eyes flashed satisfied.

"No danger," he said. "He is just unconscious. Get some water and cognac."

As one of the guards ran for what was required, the others bent over the unconscious man.

"That's Keller!" They exclaimed in unison.

"Yes, it is certainly Keller," said Krag.

"But Keller left the jail more than two hours ago."

"No," replied Krag, "he has been lying here all the time."

"But I saw him with my own eyes. I greeted him."

"In the semi-darkness of the corridor. Can you swear it was Keller?"

"The khaki suit . . ." began the other.

"Don't you understand," said Krag, "that it was the prisoner who left, Arnold Singer in Keller's suit?"

The man Krag had spoken to first intervened in the conversation.

"Now I understand what you meant by a lead," he said. "So, Arnold Singer is two hours ahead?"

Krag nodded.

The guard pointed to the unconscious man.

"Did you know about this?" he asked.

"I guessed it," replied Krag, "but I hoped for something else, and for a moment I feared the worst."

Now the jailer came with the cognac.

After a few seconds, Detective Keller opened his eyes. The first thing his distracted look met was Krag's friendly smiling face.

Suddenly Keller jumped.

"Take him!" he shouted.

Krag laid his hands reassuringly on his shoulders.

"You should have yelled that two hours ago," he said.

***

190

A few hours later, when life at the police station was in full swing, passersby could hear a lot of noise in Krag's office.

It was Keller, raging. Krag tried to calm him down, but it was not possible.

First Keller belabored himself with terrible self-reproaches, which were peppered with curses and expressions like 'idiot,' 'cattle,' 'sheep's head' and the like.

As he was trying to characterize his own behavior, Krag confined himself to occasionally inserting a tentatively contradictory, "No, no."

Finally, Keller grabbed a pile of paper from the table, tore them into many thousands of pieces, and threw them into the garbage.

"Hell and blast," he said, "there's the whole confession. Of course, it was the strange antics of the man that betrayed me. Can you believe that I, Sirius Keller, really fell into the trap, that I fell for all this waffle about psychology and motivation which no decent detective would care about in the slightest? Now I understand why there was always a lack of detail and substance in the confession. He couldn't give any proper explanations at all."

"No," said Krag, "because he has not committed any crime. His intention was to send you back and forth in your characteristic yellow khaki suit, so that everyone should believe it was you when he marched quietly through the corridor in your costume after the third or fourth pass at two o'clock in the morning. Thanks to the darkness, he succeeded as well. It was a brilliant play."

Keller grabbed his neck.

"And the man was strong."

"And knew the right grip," said Krag. "He is an anatomist. He knew what it takes to render a man unconscious."

"He had me completely fooled, believing that he was weak and sick, half dead from starvation."

"He's used to it," replied Krag.

***

At ten o'clock that same morning, Krag was admitted to Bishop de Marny's office. It was a large, elegantly appointed room with old furniture, lithographs, and books. The morning sun fell warm and bright through the open balcony door. It was the first real summer day. Beneath the windows, the park's fully unfolded trees rustled in the wind, saturating the air with fragrance. Through the transparent and bright air shone the many gilded steeples of the city.

The discreet servant, walking on noiseless soles, had left Asbjörn Krag alone in the great room. As he waited, he clearly felt the peace and harmony resting within these walls. Everything breathed silence and aristocratic seclusion, nothing seemed to belong here to the hurried and nervous present. The bookcase was full of books in dark, solid bindings. The huge mahogany desk stood on heavy feet, as if it had been planted there forever. From the gray, monochrome lithographs of the walls, past centuries looked down upon the visitor. The only thing that brightened the seriousness was a bowl of spring flowers in front of His Eminence's place. His Eminence was slow in coming.

Krag used the waiting time to study the book titles.

It was mainly scientific literature. He especially noticed a book bearing the title, *Criminal Types in Shakespeare*, by Armand Montrose. While he was still leafing through this book, His Eminence entered.

Bishop de Marny was not yet an old man. Krag had never seen him before, but he found that the bishop had something about him that reminded him of this study. Something withdrawn, distinguished, old-fashioned, with the addition of an aura of friendliness and warmth, as one often finds in truly outstanding clergy.

"I see," said His Eminence, "you hold a book written by my unfortunate friend Abbot Montrose. He belongs more to science than to the church, though I say it with regret. I believe that he has finally made his choice and chosen science. Today is the twenty-fourth. If all those strange things had not happened, I would have expected him today at this time."

"He is coming," said Krag.

XXXIX. Abbot Montrose's Fate

His Eminence asked Krag to sit down, and he sat down opposite him in his comfortable armchair.

"I am very pleased," he said, "that the energetic inquiries of the police have succeeded. If I understand you correctly, we will soon have the pleasure of seeing Abbot Montrose among us again. I hope that nothing serious has happened to him. Since you seem to think everything is already clear, is it any longer necessary for me to show you the letter that Montrose had written to me?"

"Yes," said Krag. "I came here for the letter. I think it's extremely important. I hope that something will happen during the next hour that resolves this whole matter satisfactorily. But if that something doesn't happen, I still believe the letter will be the last crucial link in my chain of evidence."

"I am genuinely pleased that you consider the letter so important," replied His Eminence with a firm smile, "then I know at least that I didn't trouble you unnecessarily."

The bishop opened his desk drawer and searched among his papers.

"The letter is totally private," he said, "therefore I doubted it would be useful to the police."

"The content is not so important, but the letter itself is."

"Ah, yes, the police understand that better than an old priest. The content is as follows," continued His Eminence, unfolding the letter. "Abbot Montrose asks me for an interview because he intends to leave the Church to devote himself entirely to his scientific studies. He asks

194

me to release him from his vows. He writes that his mind is made up and adds that there are circumstances that make a change in his decision impossible. This letter was written the evening before the horrible crimes in the Abbot's library. I confess that on previous occasions Montrose had presented me with this same plan, and that I then did what my duty required by holding him back from this sensational step. However, when I received this letter, I saw that there was no choice, for Montrose is one of those strong-willed people who cannot be dissuaded from a decision once it has been made. Therefore, I realized that there was nothing to do but dissolve his connection with the church in the most appropriate way. That is precisely the strength of our church. While our eyes are on God, we do not forget to make allowance for the inevitable events and trials of earthly life. Here's the letter, sir."

"What you have said proves to me," said Krag, "that the letter forms the final link in my chain of evidence. And I am glad that Abbot Montrose can count on a spiritual indulgence that responds to all difficulties in human life with understanding and kindness."

His Eminence bowed his head affirmatively.

Krag rushed quickly through the letter, which contained nothing more than what the bishop had already recited. Then he took from his pocket a very strong magnifying glass and the photograph of a young woman—the same photograph he had found that night in the Abbot's library. For a while he examined both the letter and the photograph very carefully through the magnifying glass.

"Do you doubt the authenticity of the manuscript?" the bishop asked.

"Oh no," replied Krag. "When Abbot Montrose wrote you this letter that evening, he accidentally got some ink on his thumb. With the help of the magnifying glass, I can examine the mark of his thumb in the lower right-hand corner of the letter. The same mark can also be found much more clearly on the back of the photograph. This photograph was found in the looted library of the Abbot. When, a few hours later, a man was suspected of the crime, his own fingerprint coincided with the mark on this photograph. Do you understand what that means?"

"Uh, no, I have to say—"

Krag placed the photograph in front of His Eminence.

"A young woman," said the bishop, "with a pretty and sympathetic face."

"Her name is Clary Singer," said Krag, "and she is responsible for the abbot's letter."

"I don't quite—"

"But," Krag continued, "so that Your Eminence gets a complete and clear picture, allow me to briefly explain. The crime caused so much publicity, which it didn't deserve, right from the start. Originally, it was nothing other than a very ordinary, badly executed break-in. The circumstances, however, meant that the one crime would entail a greater one. In general, this affair is a characteristic example of how intricate a thing can become when it becomes mingled with another, unrelated matter. The Montrose affair isn't one, but two affairs that have been running side by side, understandably confused by the public and the police. Such a thing can easily happen in a big city, where people and events cross each other without interruption. But before I continue, I must confess something to Your Eminence. I brought someone here. That someone is waiting in an adjoining room, and when the time comes, please allow me to introduce that person to Your Eminence."

"It will be my pleasure to meet the person concerned," answered the bishop in a friendly manner. "Besides, I'm very curious to hear the rest of this strange tale. Please, go on, sir."

Instead, however, Krag paused for a while, listening.

"There's a ring," he said.

"Don't let that bother you," said the bishop. "There are visitors waiting in the anteroom."

"Nonetheless, I would advise Your Eminence to inquire who has arrived."

"As you say. I understand that you have a special purpose."

He pressed the button on the desk, and after a moment a liveried servant entered. The servant's face bore the marks of extreme distraction.

"Yes, a gentleman . . . I mean, the missing one . . . I—"

"Who, my dear Morten Philipp?" The bishop asked again.

"Abbot . . . Abbot Montrose," stuttered Morten Philipp.

"Well, bring the Abbot in, man, by all means!" ordered the bishop, getting up excitedly.

Abbot Montrose entered in a black robe, such as priests wear. Big, blue lenses hid his eyes.

"Come nearer," said the bishop, "you come as a creature from beyond the grave."

Krag, too, had stood up and looked at the Abbot.

Montrose didn't move.

Then the detective walked up to him and held out his hand.

"Dear Arnold Singer," he said, "take your glasses off, the truth is out and all shall be revealed."

Abbot Montrose seemed to be fighting inside. He quickly took off his glasses and stepped firmly into the full light. It was Arnold Singer's pale face and his bright eyes that Krag had noticed from the start.

"Yes," he cried, "from now on only the truth and nothing else. I am Arnold Singer. But I'm not going back to jail."

197

"You will not," replied Krag. "The real criminals have been taken and will soon receive their punishment. I was just about to establish for His Eminence that now there is nothing else to do but practice the compassion that heals all wounds and restores happiness. You have already suffered enough due to the misunderstanding of the police. You are out of danger."

Turning to the bishop, Krag continued, "The arrival of this gentleman completes the matter. May I continue? All right, sit down, dear Abbot Montrose, my story is in many ways your story. I ask you to interrupt me when I say something that doesn't agree with the truth.

"So, gentlemen, three years ago, Abbot Montrose succumbed to the laws of life and love and married Clary Whist, daughter of the host of the Gilded Peacock."

Abbot Montrose was still silent. So, it was true.

"He had already," Krag continued, "begun a double life, perhaps not so unheard of within the priesthood as one would like to believe, satisfying his desire to live his own life, but he also protected his position outwardly as a distinguished scholar and prelate. His wife knew him only as the brave and artistic laborer who had decorated her father's hotel in such a pretty and imaginative manner. They led a perfectly happy family life. Every morning she accompanied her husband to the tram; every evening when he came home, she went to him beaming and glad. A child increased her happiness even more. I don't need to lose myself in trifles about how Abbot Montrose managed to conceal his double existence. He probably had a secret sanctuary somewhere in the city, where he daily disguised himself if his presence in the abbey apartment was not required several days in a row. I see, Abbot Montrose, that I guessed correctly. I need not mention how awfully embarrassing this double life had become over time. Science and your ministry have held you for a long time, but finally, life won, and you had decided to break your official relationship with the church. So, you turned to your friend, His Eminence, without betraying the facts of the matter. Your relationship with the church would certainly have been quietly resolved without any sensation unless an

198

unforeseen event had occurred that caused you to act swiftly, and you wrote that letter there to the bishop.

"Then it happened that crime interfered with your destiny. And the crime, in turn, threatened the discovery of your double life.

"Am I correct so far?

"Well, we've come to the evening before the robbery in your library."

XL. The Death of Arnold Singer

"But before I continue," Asbjörn Krag went on, "I must say a few words about the poor, depraved subject employed in Abbot Montrose's garden as a worker, I mean Strantz, also called the Crazy Professor. I have made further inquiries about him. He was originally intended for the priesthood and studied theology at the university. Drunkenness and hardship led him astray before he had finished his studies. He sank deeper and deeper, and when he didn't have a temporary employment, he lived with criminals and all sorts of human wreckage. But even in his deep state of humiliation, he couldn't forget the dreams of his youth and was happy when in his intoxication he could imagine for himself and others, that he had achieved the realization of his dreams. He loved playing the scholar and was happy when he could dress in some priestly robe. I have seen him in such a situation and have rarely felt the misery of a tragic life more deeply. Then it happened that this same man recognized you, Abbot, in the person of Arnold Singer. I assume it was somewhere near your house."

"It happened one morning on the tram," said the Abbot. "Without me noticing it, he followed me to my secret apartment and saw me walk away in my vestments. It was the day before the frightening event in the library."

"There we have it, and if I am not mistaken, the depraved Strantz told you what he knew the same evening and tried to extort money."

"You are not wrong."

"How did you treat him?"

"With contempt, of course. I fired him at once using the pretext that he stole flowers from the abbey garden, which he really did."

"You also paid him the remainder of his wages and wrote down the sum on a piece of paper, as was your custom."

"Yes."

"During this interview, Strantz noticed that you kept a larger sum of money in your safe."

"The hospital money, yes."

"You showed Strantz to the door with contempt, and he walked away with anger in his heart. But at the same time, you realized that your secret, which you had been so good at keeping for three years, was no longer safe. You decided it was time to cut this Gordian knot. That's why you wrote this letter to His Eminence.

"Then you went home to your wife. But now a new figure appeared on the stage, your brother-in-law, Charlie. He had just been released from prison and for various reasons, including that he feared the revenge of a fellow prisoner, wanted to and had to leave the country on the steamer the next morning. For this, he needed the sum of a thousand kroner, and you went to the abbey to gather the money he needed. It was one o'clock in the morning, and you had no qualms, protected by the darkness, about going to the abbey apartment to get the money in the library."

"I got the money and came back with it."

"But you forgot your key chain on the library table."

"Yes, unfortunately."

"And the photograph of your wife."

"It was locked in a drawer. I just took it out every now and then to look at it. I love my wife."

"Good," said Krag, "we have come so far. While you were doing all this, leaving the library, and returning to your wife, the crime that was so strangely mingled with your affair had begun elsewhere.

"Filled with grief and eager for the gold he saw in your safe, Strantz visited some of his worst acquaintances. One of whom was a recently arrived sailor of Danish descent named Hans Christian Andersen, and an old friend of the police.

"These people now decide to break into the library. They put their plan into action immediately after you left the garden. The safe was broken into and emptied, and among the booty that Strantz seized were your keys, which he imagined held much promise. Remember, he knew your secret hideaway. I suppose that only later did Strantz inform his comrades about this secret, and the criminals tried to mislead the police by imitating your handwriting and sending a letter to your lawyer, Thomas Weide."

"Yes. The criminals have been in my secret apartment, as well," snapped Montrose. "It was ransacked."

"The Crazy Professor had certainly been there," replied Krag, "for I have had the honor of seeing him perform in your vestments. It was just before he fell victim to his comrades. I, meanwhile, return to the plunder and the library.

"The policeman patrolling nearby noticed an unfamiliar noise in the library. It is probable, or rather, it is a fact that the criminals quarreled in the distribution of the spoils and engaged in a wild brawl, of which the library bears clear marks. Broken chairs, torn blankets, shattered windows. One of the thieves was punched in the nose, which left blood throughout the room. That is why it was assumed that you, Abbot, had been attacked and finally abducted, alive or dead. Meanwhile, the criminals heard the police approaching. They hurriedly wrapped the stolen goods in one of your priestly robes and climbed over the fence. A corner of the robe stuck to the iron bars of the fence, and from that it was deduced that you, Abbot, had, either voluntarily or involuntarily, taken the same route.

"Then the work of the detectives began. Our mistakes – and there were many – are to be excused by the peculiar nature of the circumstances. As it turns out, the fingerprints on the photograph are completely consistent with those of Arnold Singer, a laborer who cannot give a satisfactory explanation of his possession of a thousand kroner. Everything seems to indicate that he is the criminal. As far as Arnold Singer, the arrested gardener, is concerned, he knows that he is safe if he escapes from prison, even more so as he learns that the only man who knew his secret, the Crazy Professor, has been murdered by his accomplices for gossiping with two detectives. And that's why Singer tries to escape. The first time the attempt to escape fails, but the second time he succeeds, when with intelligence and imagination, he constructs a trap in which my capable, but somewhat naïve, friend Keller enters easily and willingly. I owe you a special greeting from him, one that I will not repeat in the presence of Your Eminence. By this time, however, I had already seen through the matter. I understood what you meant by your fantastic confession, but I had to remain patient. The matter was even then drawing to a close.

"And now," Krag concluded, and went to the door of the adjoining room, "I'll allow myself to introduce to Your Eminence the person who has accompanied me here, a poor, unhappy woman who, in the midst of her joy, has suffered a terrible blow but can now regain her happiness, by virtue of the church's compassion."

He led Clary Singer into the room.

She hurried into her husband's arms.

And here Asbjörn Krag left the reunited couple – and the astounded bishop – and returned to his life of crime.

Thanks to Bishop de Marny's care, Abbot Montrose's innocent participation in the affair remained unremarked.

Shortly thereafter, the Abbot was released from his priestly vows. He later continued his studies with great success. In particular, for someone who had led such a sheltered, religious life, he became known for an almost preternatural understanding of criminal types in Shakespeare.

Harry and Bussi were called to account for their crimes.

The Gilded Peacock was closed forever. But the Raincloud spent his last comfortable days pottering in the garden which Armand Montrose, doctor of English philosophy, established at his country estate.

Keller bought a new, unfashionably sober, suit.

And Asbjörn Krag is at work once again.

The Publisher

No, this is not another chapter of *The Final Days of Abbot Montrose*. Since you like mysteries, we've included here a short story from our book *The Adventures of Dagobert Trostler, Vienna's Sherlock Holmes* by Balduin Groller. We hope you enjoy it. But first, a word from our sponsor, which is us!

Kazabo Publishing is a new idea in the literary world. Our motto is, "Every Book a Best Seller . . . Guaranteed!" And we mean it. Our mission is to find best-selling books from around the world that, for whatever reason, have not been published in English. Sven Elvestad's novels are very popular in Europe but very few have been published in English. Why? We don't know. But we think you will agree that they should have been. And now they are.

We have found there are also many contemporary writers who are very popular in their own countries but who have not made it into English. We think this is a real shame so we are working to bring those books and those authors to you.

When you visit Kazabo.com (our website!), we hope you will always discover something new, either a book from a favorite author you didn't know existed or a completely new author with a fresh perspective from a country you admire. We promise you that everything you see with the Kazabo name – even authors you have never heard of – will be a best-seller; maybe in Italy, maybe in Japan, maybe in 1902, but a best seller. We hope you enjoy reading these literary gems as much as we enjoy finding them and bringing them to you.

But enough about us. Here is one of Dagobert Trostler's adventures entitled "The Fine Cigars."

Thanks for reading!

The Kazabo Team

Kazabo.com

The Fine Cigars

By Balduin Groller

1.

After dinner, they went into the smoking room. This was an iron law, and could not be otherwise. The two gentlemen might have preferred to sit at the table to smoke their cigars in comfort, having enjoyed the culinary masterpieces, but that was not possible, absolutely not possible. They had known this for a long time, and now the departure and exodus seemed to them quite self-evident. The beautiful housewife had made it so. In her house, smoking was allowed only in the smoking room. There, she even took part occasionally and smoked a cigarette herself in company, but for all the other rooms—she imposed this—there was the strictest ban on smoking.

Mrs. Violet Grumbach, like any self-respecting person, took as much care over her character as her apartment. Just as her outward appearance was staged with every conceivable care, with taste and good calculation, so too was the apartment. The decor was modern and expensive, everything was spick-and-span and positively sparkled in cleanliness. Yet, it is sometimes still said that former artists generally don't make good housewives!

Frau Violet had been an actress. Not one of the very foremost, but certainly one of the prettiest. Even now, all that was true! She was an exceptionally attractive woman. A little under medium height, her figure pleasingly roundish and full, already considerably more developed than at the time of her active artistry. The pale blonde hair, always elaborately ordered, bright, sparkling gray eyes, delicately drawn, soft red lips, and a piquant, pert little snub nose which still gave the round little face a kind of childish expression. All in all, a very pleasant ensemble.

At meals, she loved always to appear in a specially chosen attire. There were no children in the house, so she had time to enhance life, and overall, she had a very good way of enhancing life. She adorned herself and her surroundings. It is thus understandable that she didn't want to expose her curtains, her lace and doilies, her ceilings, and her silk carpets to the evil effects of tobacco.

Today, only one guest was present, the old friend of the house, Dagobert Trostler, and he was so at home at the Grumbach's that absolutely no bother was made on his account. If Frau Violet had once again attended elaborately to her attire, it was not actually meant for him. Once upon a time, it was customary even when she dined alone with her husband. Now, at the very most, some nuances were added on account of the guest. Thus, the heart-shaped cutout of her white lace blouse, which gave the observer some views and insights, and the half-length lace sleeves, which gave the plumpish forearms that delicately tapered to fine wrists and pretty little hands the desired scope.

Mr. Andreas Grumbach, owner of a large and very lucrative jute weaving mill, president of the General Construction Company Bank, and also bearer of numerous titles and honors, was considerably older than his wife—around twenty years or so— and if one were denied calculating the age of the ladies with too much brutal accuracy, it may be revealed with him. He might have seen fifty-three or fifty-four springs, but he looked even older than he was. His beautiful dark-brown, smooth-brushed hair proved nothing. He could have had his hair dressed professionally. His sideburns already shimmered strongly silver, and yet his chin had been shaved in the attempt to look a little younger and not to let the silvery blessing grow excessively.

Dagobert Trostler, his old friend, had by no means been sanguine when Grumbach, pursuing the late stirrings of love, had brought home the actress Violet Moorlank as his wedded spouse about six years ago. But nothing could be done about it, and finally Dagobert was proven wrong all along. A quite acceptable and respectable household developed of it. The marriage turned into a very happy one.

Dagobert himself had remained a bachelor. He was a fully-fledged man-about-town with a noticeably thinning crown and a St Peter's style tuft of hair. His Socratic face was enlivened by two dark, expressive eyes. Now he had only two great passions, music and criminology. His great fortune allowed him to devote himself to these two very divergent hobbies without any other anxiety. He had an enjoyable and creative relationship with music. His friends claimed that it was the stronger of his two talents. He, too, had known Violet when she was still a member of the theater, and when one or another of her roles required that she sing some songs, he was the one who had rehearsed her. As an amateur, of course. He remained an amateur, passionate dilettante, gentleman-rider in all the fields of activity in which he was engaged. He had, however, had some musical success with that arrangement. Indeed, in this way, he sometimes succeeded in smuggling one or another of his own compositions into the public as contributions.

As far as his criminological inclinations were concerned, they first expressed themselves in the fact that he leaned toward talking about murder-robberies and halfway respectable embezzlements. He was convinced he could have been a first-rate detective inspector, and stiffly asserted that if worst came to the worst, he would be well able to earn his bread as a detective. His friends made fun of him for it. Not that they would have doubted his talent. He had often enough provided convincing proof of that. They found only his passion for making unnecessary trouble for himself peculiar. For his hobby brought him not only numerous inconveniences, but also occasionally entangled him in really quite dangerous situations. If there was a crowd of people somewhere, he was certainly there, too, but not with an interest in the current proceedings, whatever they might be. He would watch out for pickpockets and endeavored to observe them at work and catch them in the act. For this reason, he was not infrequently involved in risky complications, but he still succeeded in delivering many a pilferer into police hands. Thus, he also loved to do research into dark crimes on his own initiative, and so it was that he brought all sorts of trouble down on his own head, had dealings in court at every moment, or was summoned to the police, to whom his private efforts had sometimes become uncomfortable. But all this gave him pleasure. He was an amateur after all.

So, one went to the smoking room.

The two gentlemen sat down at the little smoker's table near the window. Frau Violet took a seat on a small, padded bench—a very charming piece of furniture—which stretched from the high and finely structured chimney to the door, and there filled the space very becomingly. The fireplace stood in a corner, creating a very cozy little spot.

Grumbach took a cigar box from the smoking table, not at random. There were several of them there, and he had chosen carefully. He opened it and was about to pass the cigars to Dagobert as he trimmed.

"I don't know," he said thoughtfully, "there must still be a connoisseur in my house for precisely this sort of cigar. It would not be bad taste: they cost a florin apiece!"

"Do you notice disappearances?" asked Dagobert.

"I think I notice them," replied Grumbach.

"Nothing is stolen in our house," said Frau Violet, defending her honor as housewife.

"Thank God, no!" Grumbach replied. "And yet—certainly, I can't state it for a fact—but it seems to me as if only two cigars were missing from the top yesterday, and today there are eight or nine missing."

"Your own fault," remarked Dagobert. "You must simply keep them under lock and key!"

"One should be able to leave a thing lying around free in one's own home!"

"Perhaps you are mistaken?" suggested Frau Violet.

"It would not be impossible, but I don't believe it. Well, it isn't a misfortune precisely, but it is disturbing."

"It should not be difficult to get to the bottom of the matter, however," remarked Dagobert, in whom the detective passion began to stir.

"The simplest thing will be to follow your advice, Dagobert. Lock it. That's the best protection."

"That would not be interesting enough for me," was the reply. "You must catch the marten!"

"Am I supposed to be on the lookout for days on end? It'll cost me a lot less if I buy a few more cigars."

"But you must know who has access to the room."

"I stand for my servant. He takes nothing!"

"And I for my maid," Frau Violet added hurriedly. "She's been with me since I was a child, and not a pin has ever gone missing!"

"Even better," continued Dagobert. "Do you think there are daily disappearances?"

"God forbid! That's all I need! Last week I thought I had noticed it, and then perhaps in the previous week too."

The subject dropped. They spoke a little while more about the events of the day that occupied public opinion. Then the host and hostess rose to make their final preparations to attend the opera. It was their day for the box, Wednesday, and Dagobert was supposed to make one of the party, as usual. Such an old acquaintance and familiar friend of the house could be left alone for a little quarter of an hour, without awkwardness.

Frau Violet, joking, said that it must even be welcome to remain alone for a while, since he could now cogitate undisturbed on the gloomy problem of where the disappearing cigars had got to. He would surely work it out, as a master detective!

It would not have taken this mocking appeal to remind him of his hobby. He had already quietly decided to discover the perpetrator, and now he welcomed the chance to look around the scene of the crime undisturbed. The case was in fact quite insignificant, but what does an amateur not do to stay in training? He takes an opportunity like this.

When he was alone, he sat down in his armchair and began to think, for the story was not quite so simple. The last offense had been committed the day before. He assessed the cigar box and the smoking table. There was nothing to discover. It was simply disgusting what kind of cleanliness prevailed in the house, how things were tidied up and wiped down daily! How was a person expected to discover a fingerprint on the wood frame of the smoking table, which the red fabric of the ledge bordered? The frame probably was not dusty yesterday either, and since then it had been ridiculously wiped and polished again. How was a man supposed to make fingerprint studies?

Okay. Forget that.

Four electric lamps now lit the room. He turned the other eight on with a knob. Radiant light filled the room, and now he examined further. He paced the room in all directions, and sent a searching glance everywhere, unable to find any clue.

Then he sat again at the smoking table. It was clear that this had to form the center of the inquiries. However much he peered, no trace and no *corpus delicti* was discovered, But, just as he was about to resume his pacing, he noticed something. Nestled in the narrow gap between the cloth and wood frame of the smoking table, and projecting over it, was a hair, dark and shiny, not long—perhaps five centimeters, straightened—but it had the tendency to form a circle.

Dagobert ran his hand over the cloth, the frame, and the gap where the hair was. The hair bent and remained stuck. So, it had also been able to withstand polishing and dusting. On the other hand, the way things were cleaned here—absolutely disgusting—it was probably safe to assume that this resistance would hardly be permanent. Multiple attacks would probably sweep the hair away. It was quite possible, indeed probable, that it only got stuck yesterday.

212

He thought for a moment about calling in the servant to ascertain whether someone who was not part of the household had entered the room today, perhaps to get out of him who had been there yesterday, but he pushed the thought away immediately. Of course he wanted to, had to spy, but not with the servants! That could lead to foolish talk, and he was guilty of a certain regard for the house of his best friend.

So, he lifted the hair with his fingertips and put it with extreme care in his billfold. Then he continued his research. He had a good look around the entire room again. There was hardly anything more to be learned. The lighting was so bright that he was unlikely to miss anything. Up on the smooth, polished surface of the black-marble fireplace mantle, he noticed a small, dark lump interrupting the sharp straight line. Was it worth examining? For a detective, everything is worth it, anything can be worthwhile.

He pulled up a leather chair and climbed on it. A cigar butt, about four centimeters long. A very light layer of dust on the polished ledge. If only the housewife knew! It had not been wiped today. The servant had made himself comfortable. Probably he only wiped every second or third day. The thin layer of dust was not older than that. Neither was the stub. A smoker can judge these things. And another thing: there was no trace of a hand or finger on the dust surface. The ledge, therefore, had not been dusty when the cigar butt was put there. So, it had been set there yesterday.

Dagobert examined the stub. It came from the type of cigar in question.

Now Dagobert got off the chair, put the carefully wrapped stub in his pocket, extinguished the surplus lamps, and then, when the time came, went to the opera.

2.

Grumbach had already forgotten the whole cigar matter the next day. The busy factory owner and merchant had other things to think about. He didn't come back to it later, because there was no reason to do so. The matter was still not done with, however.

Dagobert let almost a whole week pass before he returned to Grumbach's home. The last time he had been there on a Wednesday, and he didn't show up again until the following Tuesday evening. Frau Violet received him in the smoking room. Dinner was over, and with the coffee he was supposed to have with her, she liked to smoke a cigarette.

"Have I arrived inopportunely, ma'am?" he began the conversation.

"You are always welcome, Herr Dagobert," she replied amiably, but she seemed to be a little bit sheepish as she sat down on the fireplace bench.

"I only meant," he went on innocently, "because I had anticipated that I would not meet your husband at home."

"Certainly, Tuesday is his club day. He is never at home then. All the more pleasant for me to have company."

"It would have been possible, however, that madame had already provided herself with different society, and that I might only have been an inconvenience."

"You are never an inconvenience, Herr Dagobert," she assured him eagerly, then steered the conversation a different direction, by attacking his weak side and beginning to tease him with his detective passion.

"Now, have you not discovered the nefarious cigar marten yet?" she asked with cheerful mockery.

"Do not mock too early, madame."

"My God, a few cigars can easily go missing without one knowing where they've gone. You should simply not investigate. The next thing will be to suspect the servant. He is certainly innocent, but once suspicion is aroused—my husband is very strict—the poor devil could easily lose his livelihood."

"We shall soon see for ourselves," replied Dagobert, pressing the electric switch.

Frau Violet was frightened by his forwardness and made a movement to hold him back, but it was already too late. In the next moment, the servant was in the room awaiting orders.

"You, my dear Franz," began Dagobert, "Will you be so good as to get me a cab, in about an hour."

"Very well, sir!"

"Here, dear friend, for your effort a fine cigar!" Dagobert reached for the little box.

"I beg your pardon, sir, I don't smoke."

"Oh, nonsense, Franz," said Dagobert. "Now get out your cigar box. We want to fill it properly." And he now reached into the little box with his whole hand.

Franz laughed broadly at the joke, and assured him that he was not a smoker.

"Well, that's all right," remarked Dagobert affably, "then we will still settle things between ourselves. You should not miss out."

The servant bowed and left the room noiselessly.

"You see, madame," resumed Dagobert. "It was not him."

Now it was up to Frau Violet to laugh brightly.

"If that's your entire trick, Dagobert, then you had better go to the bottom of the class! Indeed, I don't say that it was him—it certainly was not. But even if he had been guilty, do you really believe he would fallen into this clumsy trap?"

"Who says, Frau Violet, that this is all I have up my sleeve? I only wanted to demonstrate to you that he could not be the culprit."

"Because you believe everything he says at once. You are naïve, Dagobert."

"It was pointless for me to summon him. I only wanted to accomplish his salvation before you. Actually, in quite a superfluous way, for you, too, are convinced of his innocence, and thus we could regard the matter as closed."

"Dagobert, you know more than you say."

"I will tell you everything, if it interests you, my dear."

"I am very interested."

"Would it be better not to talk about it at all any longer?"

"Indeed, why should it be better, Dagobert?"

"I just thought—because I know everything."

"All the better. Let me hear what you have found out."

"It is, of course, possible that I am mistaken in the details, then you will be able to correct me."

"I?" She looked at him magnificently.

"You, madame. It is also possible that I will make a fool of myself—I don't believe it, but it's possible. You must take into account that I have been solely dependent on my reasoning, and I have, quite naturally, scorned to pump your servants for information."

"Not such a long introduction, Dagobert. Get to the point, please."

"Fine, I'll show my cards. You remember, my dearest, that last Wednesday I heard about the disappearances for the first time. Five minutes later I had the exact description of the person."

"How did you get that, then?"

"The exact description of the person, the smoker. I think we will stay with this designation and avoid the odious expression thief or even cigar thief. The cigars, indeed, were not stolen, but merely smoked without the master knowing it. The smoker is, therefore, a tall young man, a head taller than I am, with a well-groomed black beard and splendid teeth."

"How do you know?"

"I'll tell you everything, madame. By the way, I hope to see the correctness of the personal description I've supplied strikingly confirmed today. Namely, I reckon on the fact that the excellent young man will soon grant us the honor of his company. I have already filled the box with his favorite cigars."

Then the door opened, and the servant entered with the message that the carriage had been ordered for the gracious lord, and that it would drive up punctually at the appointed time. Then he addressed to the housewife the question of whether he was now "allowed to go." Permission was granted, and he withdrew with a submissive bow of thanks.

"Franz is actually a theater fiend," explained Frau Violet. "Once a week he must go to the theater, and I prefer to give him Tuesday evenings off, when my husband isn't at home, and he can be most easily dispensed with."

"Oh, I see," replied Dagobert thoughtfully. "Well, that is indeed fair enough."

"Do not let that distract you, dear Dagobert," continued Frau Violet. "You owe me the explanation of how you got to that description of the person."

"I had a few minutes to investigate on Wednesday, when you and your husband retired to prepare for the theater. The matter might perhaps have become difficult if I had not found any clues on the scene."

"And you found some?"

"Yes. A hair in the gap of the smoking table, and a cigar stub on the mantelpiece."

"But they could have been lying here and there for a long time!"

"I had my reasons to believe that they were actually *corpora delicti* and had only arrived there the day before. I then examined the two objects at home, the hair microscopically."

"And the result?"

"A perfectly satisfying one. The hair pointed to a perpetrator with a beautiful black beard. Natural black, no trace of artificial dye. So, an old man isn't our smoker. I can even say that it is a young man. For the hair was soft, pliant and supple. Not exactly the first fluff, but still delicate. It would have been coarser and more bristly, if a razor had prevailed there for many years past. The young man also puts something on his beard, for under the microscope the hair showed a trace of Brilliantine. This is a quite harmless, cosmetic remedy, but one must be a little vain to apply it. As you know the perpetrator, my dear, you will indeed be able to judge whether my assumption is correct or erroneous."

"I think you've gotten carried away by an obsession."

"Possibly. But that isn't important. Let's move on. Up here, on the fireplace ledge, lay the cigar stub."

"To what conclusions did it lead you?"

"First of all, I was pleased to see that the cigar type was the right one. Further conclusions were self-evident. Now allow me to return to your servant. I mention here something virtually in conclusion, which I thought and which I actually started with. Not for no reason did I call him in. You should take another look at him. So, the man is blond, and his face, as befitting a proper servant, also serving at the table, is shaved smooth. In addition, not befitting a proper servant, and as you could see for yourself when he grinned so kindly at us, he has very bad teeth. Finally, you could see that his stature is a rather small one. He's a little smaller than I am, and we have established that the unknown perpetrator has a black beard, has very good teeth, and is a head taller than I am."

"We have not yet established this at all!"

"Then we'll do so immediately. The tip of the cigar had not been cut off with a knife, but had been bitten off cleanly and smoothly. This means good teeth. Now we've got that straight. Now his unusual height must be proven. Nothing easier than that. Let us reproduce the situation, my gracious one—actually not necessary at all. Because it is already established. You at your preferred spot, I leaning against the fireplace opposite you, at a respectful distance, but still close enough for our conversation. The prospect, which I enjoy almost from a bird's eye view, is an enchanting one—you don't need to threaten, Frau Violet—an adorable one. I would not leave my happy observer post on a mere whim. But if I had to put away a cigar, I would have to go to the smoker's table, where the ashtrays stand, because I could not reach the ledge. It would be too high for me! There, now I have justified the person's description. Is it correct, my dear?"

"It is true," admitted Frau Violet, laughing. "I compliment you, Herr Dagobert. You are a terrible man, and I can see that it will be for the best if I make a comprehensive confession, or else God knows what you will believe in the end!"

"No confessions! I reject them. Confessions—of course I speak quite academically—can also be wrong. There have been legal executions on the basis of false confessions, and nothing gets my blood up more than the thought of a judicial murder. Besides, I don't need the confession. It cannot help me anymore. I am only an examining magistrate here, and I make no rulings. My task was to clarify the facts and prove the perpetrators. Whether this is confessed or denied in the final negotiation, I am not concerned."

"Good, so let us hear more!"

"So, I had to deduce further. The tall young man with the beautiful beard and the good teeth smoked his cigar here in your presence and provided you company. He chatted with you as I am now speaking with you. There could be no special secret behind it."

"Thank God that you don't think me capable of that at least, Dagobert!"

"That could not be behind it. We have known each other long enough—you are a clever woman. You know what's at stake, and you don't do stupid things."

"I thank you for your trust in my honor!"

"My trust is rock-solid, no less so my respect. But it isn't just that. I have open eyes and good ears. I myself would have noticed something, or some kind of talk would have come to me. None of any of this. You received a visit, which could not attract attention, otherwise it would have already been noticed. Why did it not attract attention? Because you often receive him. It had to have been a quite harmless visit. A circumstance, however, could make us wonder. From the explanations given by your husband, I was able to deduce that the cigars usually disappeared on Tuesday evening, at the time when he was at the club. What I didn't know, but what you indicated, is that on Tuesday your servant likes to attend the theater."

"I hope you will not draw your conclusions from this circumstance!"

"I don't think so. In fact, it seems to me that the young man appears quite frequently on the premises, but that on Tuesday he lingered a little longer and entertained the housewife."

"That is true, but I can assure that the conversations are quite harmless."

"I never doubted this, especially since the young man—how can I say? —is a little below your level."

"How did you sift that out, Dagobert?"

"It is self-explanatory, madame. Our friend Grumbach has not missed one or two cigars, but six or seven. You remember, according to him, two cigars had been missing from the top layer the day before. In any case, Grumbach took them out himself and thus half involuntarily got the impression presented by the inside of the box.

One day later, it seemed to him as if eight or nine pieces were missing. Thus, the disappearance of six or seven pieces. However, one does not smoke six or seven heavy cigars during an hour's chat with the lady of the house, one smokes one. Two at most. Now it looks as if the mistress had encouraged the young man to take a few more cigars when he left."

"That's right, too. But it still does not follow that I, as you prefer to express it, should have entertained myself with someone at a level below my own."

"I beg your pardon, my dearest. For a proper social visit, the housewife might suggest one take along a cigar—one! Of course, without emphasis. To give a handful—or to take them—well, that indicates a certain social distance."

"You are really a pure detective superintendent, Dagobert!"

"At a distance, and yet with a certain sympathy."

"He is a very nice, amiable young man. Did you uncover anything else?"

"Oh, a whole bundle! I asked myself the question: What kind of young man can come into the house so often, perhaps daily, without any sort of notice? The answer was not difficult. It could only be an official from your husband's office, probably one who has the task of bringing the cashier's key or the daily report to the boss every day."

"Certainly, after business is closed, he brings home the daily report. My husband arranged it this way."

"Which he did very correctly. I know that, too, now, by the way. Because I was recently with your director."

"The things you get up to when you follow a clue!"

"Either one doesn't begin, my dearest, or one begins, but then one must go all the way to the end. Otherwise, it's pointless."

"And what did you accomplish with the director?"

"All I could wish for."

"Let me hear about it, Dagobert!"

"I told him that I had come to patronize a young man—only he was not to betray me to the chief. The director smiled. He knew quite well that if I wanted something from the boss, it would be approved from the outset. Possibly, I admitted, but I would rather not take advantage of our friendship by asking the chief directly. The director understood, or acted as if he understood, and offered himself at my disposal.

"'What's this about?' he asked.

"'You have a young man in the office,' I replied, 'Now, what's his name? I have such a hideous memory for names! Doesn't matter; it will come. I mean a remarkably tall young man with agreeable manners'— otherwise you wouldn't have liked him, my dearest—'with a beautiful black beard and good teeth. In the evening, he usually delivers to the boss.'

"'Oh, that's our secretary, Sommer!' the director interrupted me.

"'Sommer, of course Sommer! How could the name slip my mind! You see, my dear Director, Sommer is indeed a very gifted person, but he's not at the right place in the office doing correspondence. He lacks the final precision and accuracy at work. On the other hand, he would be admirable for dealing with groups. I know that you have been looking for a suitable person for quite some time to head the sales branch in Graz. Wouldn't that be a good spot for Sommer?'

"The director slapped his forehead with his hand.

"'By goodness, that is an idea! There we are, searching until our eyes pop out of our heads and we have the man under our noses! Of course, Sommer is made for it! You haven't exercised patronage on him, rather, your suggestion does us a service. He'll go to Graz. The matter is settled.'

"You see, my dearest, I was lucky enough to be able to play God a little."

222

"But Dagobert, how could you risk the assertion that the young man is not good for the office?"

"There was no risk in it. I relied on my little bit of psychology. The right office person is always more or less—to a certain extent—a pedant. His job requires him to exercise constant minute precision. Our friend is not a pedant. The right office person doesn't bite the tips of the cigars with his teeth, but cuts them neatly with a penknife or special tool that he carries securely with him if he is a cigar smoker. And there's something else the right office person doesn't do. He doesn't put cigar butts on marble fireplaces. Instead he strives to get to the ashtray and deposits the remains there, always striving to make sure that no trace of ash is left beside it. Our careless young friend, who is imprecise with a cigar stub, probably won't be very precise with office work. He doesn't have it in him!"

"And from this, you immediately concluded that he was the right man for sales?"

"Not only from that, but from the preference you have given him, my dearest. He must be very well-spoken, and he will probably also be a bit of a ladies' man. All this is very admirable when one has to make personal contact with customers."

"One thing you must tell me, Dagobert. You have tried to get rid of the young man because you were worried about my virtue?"

"But, Frau Violet! You know what trust I place in you! But as I knew that the disappearing cigars had passed through your hands, and that you were therefore keeping a secret from your husband, the smoker really had to disappear. It had to be so!"

"A secret, yes. That was the awkwardness for me. I didn't tell my husband immediately. I didn't think of it. And if he had made an issue of it, it would have raised doubts. It would have been embarrassing to me."

"That's just as I understood it, madame. For me, by the way, my carriage must have arrived. If the young man should come to say goodbye, offer him a different variety of cigar for a change, and then this most important matter will be settled."

The End

Lightning Source UK Ltd.
Milton Keynes UK
UKHW011833260519
343347UK00001B/77/P